FIRE AND MANEUVER!

The Soviet DShK heavy machine gun opened up, and the slugs, many of them sizzling tracers, zapped through the air around Falconi's men. For the second time in the mission, Falconi and his Black Eagles faced certain death.

But Blue Richards was on the extreme right of the skirmish line. The quick-thinking navy Seal rolled out until he was free from the incoming volleys of machine gun slugs. He pulled a grenade from his patrol harness and crept toward the machine gun nest. Grasping the grenade in his right hand, he slipped the pull-ring over the muzzle of his rifle and yanked the restraining device free. Then he counted to four and hurled the grenade. The explosion kicked the big Russian gun over and shredded flesh from the NVA crew.

"C'mon, y'all!" Blue yelled, standing up. "Let's hit them sumbitches while the hittin's good!"

HO'S HELLHOUNDS

JOHN LANSING

ZEBRA BOOKS
KENSINGTON PUBLISHING CORP.

ZEBRA BOOKS

are published by

Kensington Publishing Corp.
475 Park Avenue South
New York, NY 10016

First printing: May, 1988

Printed in the United States of America

*This book is dedicated to
The United States Marine Corps
by an ex-Army Paratrooper,
with respect, and faith in the
loyalty, patriotism, and dedication
of that fine American fighting organization*

Special Acknowledgment to Patrick E. Andrews

THE BLACK EAGLES ROLL OF HONOR
(Assigned or Attached Personnel Killed in Action)

Sergeant Barker, Toby — U.S. Marine Corps
Sergeant Barthe, Eddie — U.S. Army
Sergeant Bernstein, Jacob — U.S. Marine Corps
First Lieutenant Blum, Marc — U.S. Air Force
Sergeant Boudreau, Marcel — U.S. Army
Chief Petty Officer Brewster, Leland — U.S. Navy
Specialist Four Burke, Tiny — U.S. Army
Sergeant Carter, Demond — U.S. Army
Master Sergeant Chun, Kim — South Korean Marines
Staff Sergeant Dayton, Marvin — U.S. Army
Sergeant Fotopoulus, Dean — U.S. Army
Sergeant First Class Galchaser, Jack — U.S. Army
Lieutenant Hawkins, Chris — U.S. Navy
Sergeant Hodges, Trent — U.S. Army
Mr. Hosteins, Bruno — ex-French Foreign Legion
Petty Officer Second Class Jackson, Fred — U.S. Navy
Chief Petty Officer Jenkins, Claud — U.S. Navy
Petty Officer First Class Johnson, Sparks — U.S. Navy
Specialist Four Laird, Douglas — U.S. Army
Sergeant Limo, Raymond — U.S. Army

Petty Officer Third Class Littleton, Michael —
   U.S. Navy
Sergeant Makalue, Jessie — U.S. Army
Lieutenant Martin, Buzz — U.S. Navy
Petty Officer Second Class Martin, Durwood —
   U.S. Navy
Sergeant Matsamura, Frank — U.S. Army
Staff Sergeant Maywood, Dennis — U.S. Army
Sergeant First Class Miskoski, Jan — U.S. Army
Staff Sergeant Newcomb, Thomas — Australian Army
First Lieutenant Nguyen Van Dow — South
   Vietnamese Army
Staff Sergeant O'Quinn, Liam — U.S. Marine Corps
Sergeant First Class Ormond, Norman — U.S. Army
Staff Sergeant O'Rourke, Salty — U.S. Marine Corps
Sergeant Park, Chun Ri — South Korean Marines
Sergeant First Class Rivera, Manuel — U.S. Army
Petty Officer Third Class Robichaux, Richard —
   U.S. Navy
Sergeant Simpson, Dwayne — U.S. Army
Master Sergeant Snow, John — U.S. Army
Staff Sergeant Taylor, William — Australian Army
Lieutenant Thompson, William — U.S. Navy
Staff Sergeant Tripper, Charles — U.S. Army
Staff Sergeant Valverde, Enrique — U.S. Army
First Lieutenant Wakely, Richard — U.S. Army
Staff Sergeant Whitaker, George — Australian Army
Gunnery Sergeant White, Jackson — U.S. Marine
   Corps

ROSTER OF THE BLACK EAGLES

Lieutenant Colonel Robert Falconi
U.S. Army
Commanding Officer
(15th Black Eagle Mission)

First Lieutenant Ray Swift Elk
U.S. Army
Executive Officer
(13th Black Eagle Mission)

Sergeant Major Top Gordon
U.S. Army
Operations Sergeant
(13th Black Eagle Mission)

Sergeant First Class Calvin Culpepper
U.S. Army
Demolitions Supervisor
(13th Black Eagle Mission)

Sergeant First Class Malcomb McCorckel
U.S. Army
Medical Corpsman
(13th Black Eagle Mission)

Staff Sergeant Paulo Garcia
U.S. Marine Corps
Intelligence/Communications
(5th Black Eagle Mission)

Sergeant Gunnar Olson
U.S. Army
Logistics
(3rd Black Eagle Mission)

Petty Officer 3rd Class Blue Richards
U.S. Navy
Demolitions Specialist
(8th Black Eagle Mission)

Private First Class Archie Dobbs
U.S. Army
Detachment Scout
(13th Black Eagle Mission)

CHAPTER 1

The Black Eagle Detachment had just taken one hell of a physical and emotional beating. While it was true they had emerged victorious from their latest campaign against the mad KGB Lieutenant Colonel Gregori Krashchenko and his fanatical Iron Curtain elite troops, they had paid a terrible price in blood and heartbreak. The mission had been an eyeball-to-eyeball confrontation with no quarter offered and none taken. If there had ever been a hell-on-earth, Operation Rang Dong Challenge filled the bill.

Lieutenant Colonel Robert Falconi had led a total of sixteen brave men into action in the fiery green of the Vietnam jungle. When they emerged from the Asian monsoon forest a few weeks later, Falconi had only eight with him. The missions could be described as "seek and destroy." But there was a lot more than that involved in the operation. An elite detachment of fanatically dedicated Red soldiers had broadcast a challenge to the Black Eagles to see who were the baddest bastards in Southeast Asia. The results of this man-to-man confrontation of fire and steel had been a victory, but half Falconi's command had been blown away in the fiercest fighting that the Black Eagles had been forced to endure.

In their overall history, there had been a total of forty-four out of fifty-three men killed in action. The Black Eagles had suffered a staggering eighty-three percent casualty rate. Yet the survivors' morale and dedication remained higher than could normally be expected of a decimated fighting organization. This could be traced to the personal integrity, the courage, and the fine leadership of their commander.

The detachment had been billeted out in the field for more than a year at a Special Forces "B" camp called Nui Dep. But the latest combat mission, so terribly costly, had caused the brass of the Special Operations Group to station them temporarily in Saigon out at Peterson Field. The military bureaucracy knew that even the most dedicated soldiers had morale and endurance limitations. It was felt among some staff officers that Falconi and his men were beyond what could reasonably be expected of them.

Thus, the detachment was transferred back to civilization.

There, in a special fortified Saigon barracks surrounded by the defensive guns of an ARVN heavy weapons infantry oufit, the nine survivors spent a quiet time recovering from the ordeal. Mostly they just drank beer and helped each other step by step to as normal a mental condition as could be expected of them. Most preferred this temporary monastic existence, with an occasional trip into town for casual feminine companionship. But three had close personal relationships with specific women.

Falconi himself was back with the beautiful Eurasian Andrea Thuy in their hot, passionate on-again-off-again romance. Andrea was also a Black Eagle and had participated in several campaigns in which she had held her own in combat. But her love affair with Falconi had caused the CIA case officer Chuck Fagin to have her removed from active field service and assigned as his administrative assistant at Peterson Field. Emotional entanglements cause bad judgments where snap decisions involving life and death must be made. So now, instead of fighting side by side with her man, Andrea saw him during the times he was in from the field.

Malpractice McCorckel had the most serious and permanent relationship with the opposite sex. He was a married man and went to stay with his Vietnamese wife, Jean, in their apartment. Archie Dobbs's romance was almost as ardent. He was deeply in love, spending what free time he had with his girlfriend Betty Lou Pemberton, who was an army nurse.

But, no matter whether they stayed in a self-imposed exile or went out to seek female companionship, the Black Eagles remained their individualistic selves, each man unique unto himself.

There was First Lieutenant Ray Swift Elk. This full-blooded Sioux Indian was lean and muscular. His copper-colored skin, hawkish nose, and high cheekbones gave him the appearance of the classic prairie warrior. The great artists of the American West, Remington and Russell, could have used him as the perfect model in their portrayals of the noble Red Man. Ray Swift Elk had one hell of an army service record. As a matter of fact, there were still dark spots on his fatigues where he'd removed his master sergeant chevrons after his battlefield commission. Brand new cloth insignia of an infantry lieutenant were sewn on his collars.

Twelve years of service in Special Forces had made Swift Elk particularly well qualified to be the detachment executive officer. This particular position was important because, in reality, he was Falconi's second in command.

In spite of his skills and his education in modern soldiering, Swift Elk still considered his ancestral past an important part of his life, and he practiced Indian customs when and where able. Part of his tribe's history included some vicious combats against the black troopers of the U.S. Cavalry's 9th and 10th Cavalry Regiments of the racially segregated army of the nineteenth century. The Sioux warriors had nicknamed the black men they fought "Buffalo Soldiers." This was because of their hair, which, to the Indians, was like the thick manes on the buffalo. The appellation was a sincere compliment, coming from these native Americans' veneration of the bison. Ray Swift Elk called Calvin Culpepper, the black guy in the detachment, "Buffalo Soldier," and he did so with the same respect his ancestors demonstrated toward Uncle Sam's black horse troopers during the violent Plains Wars.

The next man in the Black Eagle chain of command was Sergeant Major Top Gordon. As the senior noncommissioned officer of the Black Eagles, he was tasked with several administrative and command responsibilities. Besides having to take any issued operations plans and use them to form the basic operations orders for the missions, he was also responsible for maintaining discipline and efficiency within the unit.

Top was a husky man, his jet-black hair thinning perceptibly, looking even more sparse because of the strict G.I. haircut he wore. His entrance into the Black Eagles had been less than satisfactory. After seventeen years spent in the army's elite spit-and-polish airborne infantry units, he had brought in an attitude that did not fit well with the diverse individuals in Falconi's command. Gordon's zeal to follow army regulations to the letter had cost him a marriage when his wife, fed up with having a husband who thought more of the army than her, filed for divorce and took their kids back to the old hometown in upstate New York. Despite that heartbreaking experience, he hadn't let up a bit. To make the situation even more difficult for him during his first days in the Black Eagles, he had taken the place of a popular detachment sergeant who was killed in action on the Song Bo River. This noncom, called "Top" by the men, was an old Special Forces man who knew how to handle the type of soldier who volunteered for unconventional units. Any new top sergeant would have been resented no matter what type of man he was.

Gordon's premier appearance in his new assignment brought him into quick conflict with the Black Eagle personnel. Within only hours, the situation had gotten so far out of hand that Falconi began seriously to consider relieving the sergeant and seeing to his transfer back to a regular airborne unit.

But during Operation Laos Nightmare, Gordon's bravery under fire had earned him the grudging respect of the lower-ranking Black Eagles. Finally, when he fully realized the problems he had created for himself, he'd changed his methods of leadership. Gordon backed off doing things by the book and found he could still maintain good discipline and efficiency while getting rid of the chicken-shit aspects of army life. It was finally apparent he had been accepted by the men when they bestowed the nickname "Top" on him.

He had truly become the "top sergeant" then. But his natural gruffness and short temper remained the same. Nothing could change those characteristics.

The detachment medic, Sergeant First Class Malcomb "Malpractice" McCorckel, an original member of the unit, was always right on Top Gordon's heels. An inch under six feet in height, Malpractice had been in the army for twelve years. He had a friendly face and spoke softly as he pursued his duties in seeing after the illnesses and hurts of his buddies. He nagged and needled each and every one of them in order to keep that wild bunch healthy. They bitched back at him, but not angrily, because each Black Eagle appreciated the medical sergeant's concern. They all knew that nothing devised by puny man—not even mortar fire or grenades—could keep Malpractice from reaching a wounded detachment member and pulling him back to safety. Malpractice was unique in the unit for another reason, too. He was the only married man under

16

Falconi's command.

The detachment's slowest, easiest-going guy, Petty Officer Blue Richards, was a fully qualified Navy Seal. Besides his fighting skills, his special claim to fame was his uncanny tree-climbing ability. When it was necessary to go high to get a good look around, Blue could be counted on to shinny up even the tallest trees. A red-haired Alabamian with a gawky, good-natured grin common to good ol' country boys, Blue had been named after his "daddy's favorite huntin' dawg." An expert in demolitions either on land or underwater, Blue considered himself honored that his father had given him that dog's name.

Then there was Marine Staff Sergeant Paulo Garcia. Under the new reorganization of the detachment that was necessary after suffering such heavy casualties, Paulo performed both the communications and intelligence work for the Black Eagles. Of Portuguese descent, this former tuna fisherman from San Diego, California, had joined the Marines at the relatively late age of twenty-one after deciding to look for a bit of adventure. There was always Marine Corps activity to see around his hometown, and he decided that that fighting group offered him exactly what he was looking for. Ten years of service and plenty of combat action in the Demilitarized Zone and Khe Sanh made him more than qualified for the Black Eagles.

Sergeant First Class Calvin Culpepper was a tall, brawny black man who had entered the army off a poor Georgia farm his family had worked as sharecroppers. Although once a team leader in the detachment, the new set-up got him back to his usual job of handling all the senior demolition chores. His favorite tool in that line of work was C4 plastic explosive. It was said he could set off a charge under a silver dollar and get back ninety-nine cents change. Resourceful, intelligent, and combatwise, Calvin, called the "Buffalo Soldier" by Lieutenant Ray Swift Elk, pulled his weight—and then a bit more—in the dangerous undertakings of the Black Eagles.

The newest man was army Sergeant Gunnar Olson who had officially taken part in one Black Eagle mission before his actual assignment to the detachment. This had been during the operation on the Song Cai River when he'd been a gunner—appropriately called Gunnar the Gunner—on a helicopter gunship that flew fire support operations for Falconi and his men. Gunnar was so impressed with the detachment that he immediately put in for a transfer to the unit. Falconi quickly approved the paperwork and hired Gunnar the Gunner on as the unit's heavy weapons man. Now armed with an M70 grenade launcher and a .45 caliber automatic pistol, Gunnar, of Norwegian descent and from Minnesota, looked forward to continued service with the detachment, despite the mauling they'd taken on their last mission.

The man with the most perilous job in the detachment was PFC Archie Dobbs, and no other unit in the army had a man quite like him. Formerly a brawling, beer-swilling womanizer, Archie had been a one-man public scandal and disaster area in garrison or in town. But that was before he'd found his new love, army nurse Betty Lou Pemberton. Now his wild ways had tamed down quite a bit. But, out of control or not, once Archie was out in the field he was point man and scout. In that job he went into the most dangerous areas first.

That was his trade: to see what—or who—was there. Reputed to be the best compass man in the United States Army, his seven years of service were fraught with stints in the stockade and dozens of "busts" to lower rank. Fond of women and booze, Archie's claim to fame—and the object of genuine respect from the other men—was that he had saved their asses on more than one occasion by guiding them safely through throngs of enemy troops behind the lines. Like the cat who always landed on his feet, Archie could be dropped into the middle of any geographic hell and find his way out. His sense of direction was flawless and had made him the man of the hour on several Black Eagle missions during dangerous exfiltration operations when everything had gone completely and totally to hell.

After a couple of weeks of their quiet stay at Peterson Field, the Black Eagles began to drift back to their old selves. Blue Richards and Calvin Culpepper were the first to leave the barracks. The pair went into town, and though they didn't raise hell in the usual way, they kicked back a bit and enjoyed a few beers and sought out some bar girls to relieve the heavy physical needs that had built up in them.

Ray Swift Elk accompanied Falconi on a couple of debriefing sessions at SOG headquarters, and the extra work seemed to clear his head a bit.

Top Gordon, a close friend of the McCorckels', had dinner at their apartment a couple of times. It was actually Paulo Garcia and Gunnar the Gunner Olson who blew off the first cloud of steam. The pair hit Saigon and went on a satisfying, shit-kicking drunk that left them both with monumental hangovers.

By the time Archie Dobbs had managed to get into a big argument with Betty Lou, things were really back to normal. Falconi sensed this and began a training regimen that included some heavy physical workouts and predawn runs. After starting their workday with that bit of an eye-opener, they spent the rest of the daily training in "skull practice," going over hypothetical tactical situations and working out the solutions. There was also some hard preventive maintenance and repair on their weaponry, and finally a trip out to an ARVN rifle range to sharpen up any slackening off of their shooting abilities.

Any other emotional pressures or frustrations were worked out in the hand-to-hand combat training as the Black Eagles slammed each other around in a combination of karate, judo, and street-brawling drills.

One late afternoon, after a particularly vigorous workout, the nine men had pounded each other black and blue. They were ending the training day with a few cold beers out of the cooler kept in their billets.

They all snapped their eyes toward the entrance of the building when Chuck Fagin banged the door open. He stepped into the room and stood there momentarily with his battered old canvas briefcase held in front of him.

Archie Dobbs took a swig of beer. "You look like a man with a purpose, Chuck."

"I am," Fagin replied.

Calvin Culpepper wiped at the sweat streaking down his face. "I see you got that ol' bag o' yours, Fagin. Does that mean what I think it does?"

Fagin smiled sardonically. "Just what the hell do you guys think it means?"

Blue Richards took a deep breath. "Is there an OPLAN in there?"

"You bet your sweet ass there is," Fagin said. "Vacation is over, kiddies," he said, walking across the room to the table on the other side of the bunks. He pulled the operation plan from the bag. "They're calling this one 'Operation Hellhound.'"

CHAPTER 2

The acronym OPLAN, used by Chuck Fagin to refer to the papers in his briefcase, stood for Operations Plan.

An OPLAN is a brief concept of how a scheduled operation or mission should be conducted. The particular one that Fagin carried into the billets at Peterson Field had been aptly designated—as he had told the Black Eagles—OPLAN Operation Hellhound. This document was written by the staff at Special Operations Group on the other side of that same Peterson Field. That particular team of officers wanted a specific job carried out. Even at that high echelon level, it was not considered to be "etched in stone." Instead, it was actually a set of guidelines and information supplied to Lieutenant Colonel Robert

23

Falconi and his men so that they could assimilate the information supplied and add their own input along with other data to create another, much more authoritative paper that would be called the OPORD (Operation Order).

The OPORD was written along strict guidelines that divided it into five basic paragraphs, as follows:

1. SITUATION

a. Enemy Forces: (This was the strength, activity, identification, etc. of the bad guys that Falconi and his men were going to face.)

b. Friendly Forces: (These were the good joes that would be participating—or at least be located damned close—to them during Operation Hellhound. This included special notes on support capabilities, coordination, cooperation, etc. In most Black Eagle missions this paragraph was labeled "N/A"—Not Applicable— since the detachment would be out in the boonies, operating on their own.)

2. MISSION

(A simple statement saying exactly what the Black Eagles were supposed to accomplish.)

3. EXECUTION

a. Concept of the Operation: (The "How-It's-Gonna-Be-Done" paragraph, which included times, dates, organization, specific duties, etc.)

4. ADMINISTRATION AND LOGISTICS

a. Rations

b. Arms and Ammunition

c. Uniforms and Equipment

d. Special (Handling of wounded, prisoners, etc.)

5. COMMAND AND SIGNAL
  a. Signal: (Equipment, call signs, etc.)
  b. Command: (The chain of command).

Falconi walked over to the table and read Fagin's OPORD. Then he looked further into the CIA officer's briefcase and found seventeen more copies. "Why so many?" he asked. "There're only nine of us."

Fagin sighed. "The dumb sons of bitches still have standing orders to issue seventeen. They know there were eight casualties on the last mission, but some admin snafu has kept the word from actually being put down on paper so they don't take that into consideration. Their SOP says make up seventeen copies, so that's the number of copies the clerks run off on their mimeograph machine."

"Being a paperwork commando is pure hell, isn't it?" Falconi said. He turned to his men. "I don't know what the hell you're standing around for looking so dumb and happy. Hasn't it sunk into your thick skulls yet? It ought to be obvious as hell that there's a mission going down." He perused the OPORD again. "And according to this, its D-Day is seventy-two short hours away."

"Shit!" Malpractice, the married man, said. "When do we go into Isolation?"

"You're in it now," Fagin said. "Don't worry, Malpractice. Andrea is going over to tell Jean about it." He looked at Archie. "She'll tell Betty Lou, too."

"Hey!" Calvin hollered happily. "There's two bar girls downtown that oughta be told about me and Blue."

"You lover boys go into Isolation on the Q.T.,"

Fagin said. "Anyhow, if the army sent out official notification to the kind of women you two hang around with, they'd be representing half the armed forces of the world."

"Hey!" Blue said, feigning shocked indignation. "Are you saying our women is loose?"

"Loose?" Fagin said, guffawing. "A hundred yards of G.P. strap couldn't hold 'em together."

Blue grinned. "When you're right, you're right, Fagin."

"Awright! Can the joking!" Sergeant Major Top Gordon said. The top enlisted man of the detachment, who had been uncharacteristically quiet the previous weeks, suddenly became the senior noncommissioned officer again. "What the fuck are you jokers waiting for? Knock off the bullshit and hit the showers and get ready to go to work. This ain't a goddamned R&R, it's Isolation!"

The men jumped to life as Lieutenant Colonel Robert Falconi and Lieutenant Ray Swift Elk went off into a corner to huddle with Fagin and brainstorm the mission that lay ahead.

The term "Isolation" described accurately and precisely the new status of the detachment. They were literally isolated from the outside world. In order to insure complete and certain security, no one—not even their families or closest friends—would be permitted any contact from them. This extended to other members of the military, with Operation Hellhound officially put under a classification of SNTK—Special Need To Know.

Within a half hour every man was showered and changed into a fresh uniform. Top Gordon passed out individual copies of the OPLAN. As each man received his, he went to his area in the billets. Here there were more than his uniforms, weapon, bunk, and equipment issue. There were also a table, chair, and portable G.I. typewriter with plenty of paper.

Within a few moments, the writing machines were clacking away as the men began composing the annexes for which they were personally responsible.

The overall concept belonged to Ray Swift Elk and Top Gordon. After reading the basic document, they drew up the plans that the pair would present to Falconi for approval. That was what an operations officer and sergeant did in a combat situation. They planned the methods to be used in accomplishing the assigned mission. Their ideas, of course, were dependent on the approval of the commander, but the basic concept of how to do the thing was theirs.

Calvin Culpepper and Blue Richards were listed as demolitions men, but another title that fit them was engineer. Their particular annex, therefore, had to do with any necessary building or erecting of fortifications, bridges, trails, and other needed construction jobs. On the other side of the coin, of course, was the type of work they enjoyed the most: the complete and utter destruction of such items.

Malpractice McCorckel was concerned with the medical aspects of the operation. This quite complicated area included treatment of wounded, sanitation, and the prevention of illness. His annex would include information on diseases in the area of operation, special health problems, as well as the evacuation of casualties.

Information on the enemy and communications had

27

been dumped in Paulo Garcia's lap. He had to find out all he could about enemy units, operations, and potentials in the area, then make sure the other Black Eagles were brought up to date on this vital information.

Gunnar Olson would really be running his ass off. Not only was he charged with forecasting the supply needs for the mission, the poor guy had actually to go draw the items from G4. This meant, at least, that he was allowed to leave Isolation now and then to tend to these chores. It was a small blessing, however, since he would get the least sleep of anyone, with the exception of the commander, Robert Falconi.

Archie Dobbs pored over maps of the operation area, familiarizing himself with every ridge line, swamp, hill, and other terrain features where they would be fighting. In official parlance, what he was doing was called "reconnaissance by map." Since he was the man who would lead the way from one objective to the other, he had to do the job flawlessly and quickly. Any stumbling and bumbling by getting lost or going the wrong way could cause failure of the mission—which translated into living or dying where the Black Eagles were concerned.

The billets fairly hummed with activity. Falconi got his information by grilling Fagin who, in his turn, had put some hapless SOG officer through his own brand of third degree to get the scoop on the situation.

"How reliable is this ARVN unit we're going to use?" Falconi asked.

"A damned fine ranger outfit," Fagin answered. "Their commander has proven himself time and time

28

again. His men are dedicated and loyal to him."

"What about Americans like us tagging along?" Falconi inquired. "Won't that raise suspicions, or at least unusual interest?"

Fagin shook his head. "No way. Most of their work has been with U.S. advisors, so you guys shouldn't rate a second look."

"Yeah? Does that include Viet Cong spies loitering around the area?"

"Sure," Fagin assured him. "They've seen the Americans, too."

Paulo Garcia left his typewriter and approached them. "Are the Viet Cong units in the O.A. working with any NVA at this particular time?"

"Negative," Fagin said. "Everything that G2 has come up with shows the area is pure V.C. turf."

"Okay," Paulo said. "Is their commo gear any good if ours goes out?"

Fagin shook his head. "It's a pretty primitive operation over there, Paulo. About the only thing the enemy is going to be good for in commo is signal flags and crude lanterns."

"Okay," Paulo said. "Thanks, Chuck."

Before Falconi and Fagin could start talking again, Malpractice McCorckel came up to them. "Archie tells me there's plenty of swamps and ponds on the map. What's the mosquito situation out there?"

"It's no worse—or better—than anyplace else," Fagin said. "But it doesn't look like you'll be having any particular problems."

"Okay." Malpractice wandered back to his area.

Falconi lit a cigarette. "How much backing can you

promise us?"

"I'll be on the scene," Fagin said. "And so will Andrea."

"Will you be working with that sonofabitch Taggart?" Falconi asked.

"He's the boy that calls the shots," Fagin conceded. "And I gotta level with you, Falconi. The guy isn't bothered by casualty rates. As far as Brigadier General Taggart is concerned, the last operation against Krashchenko and his fanatics was an unqualified success."

"Despite fifty percent casualties in my command?" Falconi asked angrily. "The guy worries me, Fagin. Every time we go out, I expect to find myself on a suicide mission."

"I know where you're coming from," Fagin said. "But with Andrea helping me, we can keep a real handle on the situation." He leaned forward, his face showing the concern he felt. "You gotta trust us, Falconi. We're bucking a hell of a bureaucratic system, but we won't let you down."

"I'm not worried about you," Falconi said. "What bothers me is the shit that Taggart dreams up for us."

They were interrupted again, this time by Gunnar Olson. "Hey, Fagin, there ain't any heavy weapons on the table of allowances for this operation."

"The idea is for you to travel light," Fagin said.

"How about one machine gun, or at least some grenade launchers?" Gunnar asked.

"Sorry."

"Uff da!" Gunnar said in Norwegian. "You know me, Fagin. I like big guns around."

"It'll just be M16s this trip," Fagin said. "By the way,

30

will you be able to draw the rations with me in a couple of hours?"

"I guess I'd better be," Gunnar said, walking away. "You know where to find me."

Falconi lit another cigarette. He took a drag and looked at the burning butt between his fingers. "I have to give these damned things up."

Fagin pulled a large cigar from his jacket pocket. "I ain't giving up nothing, man. Not my stogies and certainly not my Irish whiskey."

"I admire a man of conviction," Falconi said. He turned and looked over at his men on the other side of the building. Each was lost in his work, knowing the importance of doing a thorough, accurate job on the individual annexes. "Now those—" he said, pointing at the detachment—"are men of conviction."

"A man has lots of conviction," Fagin said, "especially when he knows he'll die if he fucks up."

"Good point," Falconi replied.

Gunnar returned. "I want binoculars for everybody," he said.

"Good idea," Falconi said. He looked at Fagin. "Well?"

"You got 'em."

"And hammocks with mosquito netting," Gunnar added. "Malpractice said they gotta have mosquito netting."

"I presume you're talking about the kind that roll up into little balls and you can stuff in your patrol pack," Fagin said.

"Yeah."

"You got 'em."

Gunnar nodded and returned to his paperwork.

"You're all heart, Fagin," Falconi said.

"Just fill out the proper requisitions," Fagin reminded them.

Falconi started to light another cigarette off the one he was finishing. Instead he ground the lit one out in the ashtray in front of him. "These things definitely aren't good for your health."

"Neither is getting hit in the head by an AK47 bullet," Fagin said.

32

CHAPTER 3

The Black Eagles had not suddenly sprung into being.
On the other hand, they were not a slowly evolving old
established unit with years of tradition behind them,
either.

In reality, they were the brainchild of a Central
Intelligence Agency case officer named Clayton
Andrews. But his creation of the detachment was not
an easy process by any means. His initial plans to
activate the unit were met with the usual stodgy, stupid
resistance that military bureaucrats—like all bureaucrats—give to any innovative new ideas. But Clayton
Andrews was not the kind of individual to take such
mindless rebuffs kindly.

That man growled and kicked through knotted red

tape for months before he finally received the official okay to turn his concept of creating an independent band of jungle fighters into a living, breathing, ass-kicking reality.

In those early days of the 1960s, "Think Tanks" of Ph.D.s at various centers of American political thought and study were conducting mental wrestling matches with the question of fighting Communism in southeast Asia. The threat of this ideology spreading in that part of the world was very real indeed. Powerful people in the United States government were concerned enough to see that some of the best brains in the country were assigned to come up with a solution on containing this political and military force.

Andrews was involved in that same program, but in a tremendously more physical way than the brainy types. His work was in marked contrast to their efforts. His method of handling the situation was not intellectual, it was purely physical.

He was in combat.

And the CIA man participated in more than just a small amount of clandestine fighting in Cambodia, Laos, and Vietnam. He hit it in a big way, which included a hell of a lot of missions that went beyond mere harassment operations in Viet Cong and Pathet Lao areas. His main job was the conduct of penetrations into North Vietnam itself. Over a very short period of time this dangerous assignment cost plenty of good men their lives, because some of the personnel involved, no matter how dedicated or brave, were not the proper men for such a dangerous undertaking. The appalling casualty rate motivated Andrews to begin his battle with the stodgy military administration to set things up properly.

It took diplomatic persuasion—combined with a few ferocious outbreaks of temper—before the program was eventually expanded. When the final approval was granted, Andrews was suddenly thrust into a position where he needed not simply an *excellent* combat commander, he needed the *best*. Thus, he began an extensive search for an officer to lead that special detachment needed to carry out certain down-and-dirty missions.

There were months of personnel investigations and countless interviews with hopeful contenders for the job. In the end, after exhaustive effort, Andrews settled on a Special Forces captain named Robert Falconi.

Pulling all the strings he had, Andrews saw to it that the Green Beret officer was transferred to his own branch of SOG—the Special Operations Group—to begin work on this brand new project.

Captain Falconi, immediately upon his arrival from his Special Forces detachment, was tasked with organizing a new fighting unit to be known as the Black Eagles. This group's basic policy was to be primitive and simple, and Falconi summed it up in his own words: "Seek out the enemy and kill the sons of bitches."

Their mission was to penetrate deep into the heartland of the Communists, to disrupt, destroy, maim, and slay. The men who would belong to the Black Eagles would be volunteers from every branch of the armed forces. And that was to include all nationalities involved in the struggle against the Red invasion of South Vietnam.

Each man was to be an absolute master in his

particular brand of military mayhem. He had to be an expert in not only his own nation's firearms but also in those of other friendly and enemy countries. But the required knowledge in weaponry didn't stop at the modern types. It included acquaintance with knives, bludgeons, garrotes, and even crossbows, should the need to deal silent death arise.

Additionally, there was a requirement for the more sophisticated and peaceful skills. Foreign languages, land navigation, communications, medical skills, and even mountaineering and scuba diving were to be within the realm of knowledge of the Black Eagles. Then, in addition, each man was to know how to type. In an outfit that had no clerks, this office skill was extremely important, because of each having to do his own paperwork. Much of this consisted of the operations orders that directed their highly complicated, dangerous missions. These documents had to be legible and easy to read in order to avoid confusing, deadly errors in combat.

Now it was Falconi who combed through 201-files and called up men for interviews. Some he had served with before, others he knew by reputation, while there were also hundreds whose military records reflected their qualifications. Scores were interviewed, but in the end only a dozen were selected.

They became the enforcement arm of SOG, drawing the missions that were the most dangerous and sensitive. In essence they were hit men, closely coordinated and completely dedicated, held together and directed through the forceful personality of their leader, Captain Robert Falconi.

Finally, as happens to all good men, Clayton

Andrews had done his job too well. Despite his protests, he was promoted out of the job. Immediately a new CIA officer moved in. This was Chuck Fagin. An ex-paratrooper and veteran of both World War II and the Korean War, Fagin had a natural talent when it came to dreaming up nasty things to do to the unfriendlies up north. It didn't take him long to get Falconi and his boys busy.

Their first efforts were directed against a pleasure palace in North Vietnam.[1] This bordello *par excellence* was used by Communist officials during their retreats from the trials and tribulations of administering authority and regulation over their slave populations. These Red hotshots found that there were no excesses, perverted tastes or unusual demands that went unsatisfied in this hidden fleshpot.

Falconi and his wrecking crew sky-dived into the operational area in a HALO (High Altitude Low Opening) infiltration, and when the Black Eagles finished their raid on the whorehouse, there was hardly a soul left alive to continue the debauchery.

Their next hell-trek into the enemy's hinterlands was an even more dangerous assignment, with the difficulty factor multiplied by the special demands placed on them.[2] The North Vietnamese had set up a special prison camp in which they were perfecting their skills in the torture-interrogation of downed American pilots. With the conflict escalating in Southeast Asia, they rightly predicted that they would soon have more than just a few Yanks in their hands. A North Korean brainwashing expert had come over from his native

[1] Black Eagles No. 1—*Hanoi Hellground*
[2] Black Eagles No. 2—*Mekong Massacre*

country to teach them the finer points of mental torment. He had learned his despicable trade during the Korean War when he had had American POWs directly under his control. His use of psychological torture, combined with just the right amount of physical torment, had broken more than one man, despite the most spirited resistance. Experts who studied his methods came to the conclusion that only a completely insane prisoner, whose craziness caused him to abandon both the sensation of pain and the instinct for survival, could have resisted the North Korean's methods.

At the time of the Black Eagles' infiltration into North Vietnam, the prisoners behind the barbed wire were few—but important. A U.S.A.F. pilot, an army Special Forces sergeant, and two high-ranking officers of the South Vietnamese forces were the unwilling tenants of the concentration camp.

Falconi and his men were not only required to rescue the POWs, but also had to bring along the prison's commandant and his North Korean tutor. Falconi had pulled off the job, fighting his way south through the North Vietnamese army and air force to a bloody showdown on the Song Bo River. The situation had deteriorated to the point where the Black Eagles' magazines had had their last few rounds in them as they waited for the NVA's final charge. But the unexpected but spirited aid from anti-Communist guerrillas had turned the tide, and the Black Eagles smashed their way out of the encirclement.

The next operation took them to Laos, where they were pitted against the fanatical savages of the Pathet

Lao.[3] If that wasn't bad enough, their method of entrance into the operational area was bizarre and dangerous. Their type of transport into battle hadn't been used in active combat in more than twenty years. It had even been labeled obsolete by military experts. But this hadn't deterred the Black Eagles.

They used a glider to make a silent flight to a secret landing zone. If that wasn't bad enough, the operations plan called for their extraction through a glider-recovery apparatus that not only hadn't been tested in combat, but had never been given sufficient trial under rehearsed, safe conditions.

After a hairy ride in the flimsy craft, they hit the ground to carry out a mission designed to destroy the construction site of a Soviet nuclear power plant the Reds wanted to install in the area. Everything went wrong from the start, and the Black Eagles fought against a horde of insane zealots until their extraction to safety. This was completely dependent on the illegal and unauthorized efforts of a dedicated U.S.A.F. pilot—the same one they had rescued from the North Vietnam prison camp. The air force colonel was determined to help the men who had saved him, and he came through with all pistons firing, paying the debt he owed Falconi's guys.

This hairy episode was followed by two occurrences: The first was Captain Robert Falconi's promotion to major, and the second was a mission that was doubly dangerous because of the impossibility of making firm operation plans. Unknown Caucasian personnel, posing as U.S. troops, had been committing atrocities

[3] Black Eagles No. 3—*Nightmare In Laos*

against Vietnamese peasants.[4] The situation had gotten far enough out of control that the effectiveness of American efforts in the area had been badly damaged. Once again Falconi and the Black Eagles had been called in to put things right. They had gone in on a dark beach from a submarine and begun a determined reconnaissance until they finally made contact with their quarry.

These enemy agents, wearing U.S. army uniforms, were dedicated East German Communists prepared to fight to the death for their cause. The Black Eagles admired such unselfish dedication to the extent that they gave the Reds the opportunity to accomplish that end: Sacrifice their lives for Communism.

But this wasn't successfully concluded without the situation deteriorating to the point where the Black Eagles had to endure human-wave assaults from a North Vietnamese army battalion led by an infuriated general. This officer had been humiliated by Falconi on the Song Bo River several months previously. The mission ended in another Black Eagle victory, but not before five more good men had died.

Brought back to Saigon at last, the seven survivors of the previous operations cleaned their weapons, drew fresh, clean uniforms, and prepared for a long-awaited period of R&R—Rest and Recreation.

It was not to be.

Chuck Fagin's instincts and his organization of agents had ferreted out information that showed a high-ranking intelligence officer of the South Vietnamese army had been leaking information on the Black Eagles to his superiors up in the Communist

[4] Black Eagles No. 4—*Pungi Patrol*

north.[5] It would have been easy enough to arrest this double agent, but an entire enemy espionage net had been involved. Thus, Falconi and his Black Eagles had to come in from the boondocks and fight the good fight against these spies and assassins in the back streets of Saigon itself.

When Saigon was relatively cleaned up, the Black Eagles drew a mission that involved going out on the Ho Chi Minh trail on which the North Vietnamese sent supplies, weapons, and munitions south to be used by the Viet Cong and elements of the North Vietnamese army.[6] The enemy was enjoying great success, despite repeated aerial attacks by the U.S. and South Vietnamese air forces. The high command decided that only a sustained campaign conducted on the ground would put a crimp in the Reds' operation.

Naturally, they chose the Black Eagles for the dirty job.

Falconi and his men waged partisan warfare in its most primitive and violent fashion, with raids, ambushes, and other forms of jungle fighting. The order of the day was "kill or be killed" as the monsoon forest thundered with reports of numerous types of modern weaponry. This dangerous situation was made even more deadly by a decidedly insidious and deadly form of mine warfare, which made each track and trail through the brush a potential zone of death.

When this was wrapped up, Falconi and his troops received an even bigger assignment. This next operation involved working with Chinese mercenaries to secure an entire province ablaze with infiltration and

[5] Black Eagles No. 5—*Saigon Slaughter*
[6] Black Eagles No. 6—*AK47 Firefight*

invasion by the North Vietnamese army.[7] This even involved beautiful Andrea Thuy, a lieutenant in the South Vietnamese army who had been attached to the Black Eagles. Playing on the mercenaries' superstitions and religion, she became a "warrior-sister," leading some of the blazing combat herself.

An affair of honor followed this mission, when Red agents kidnapped this lovely woman.[8] They took her north—but not for long. Falconi and the others pulled a parachute-borne attack and brought her out of the hellhole where her Communist tormentors had put her.

The ninth mission, pulled off with most of the detachment's veterans away on R&R, involved a full-blown attack by North Vietnamese regulars into the II Corps area—all the while saddled with a pushy newspaper reporter.[9]

By that time South Vietnam had rallied quite a number of allies to her side. Besides the United States, there were South Korea, Australia, New Zealand, the Philippines, and Thailand. This situation had upset the Communist side, and they had decided to counter it by openly having various Red countries send contingents of troops to bolster the NVA (North Vietnamese Army) and the Viet Cong.

This had resulted in a highly secret situation—ironically well known by both the American and Communist sides—which developed in the borderland between Cambodia and South Vietnam.[10] The Reds, in an effort to make their war against the Americans

---

[7] Black Eagles No. 7—*Beyond the DMZ*
[8] Black Eagles No. 8—*Boocoo Death*
[9] Black Eagles No. 9—*Bad Scene At Bong Son*
[10] Black Eagles No. 10—*Cambodia Kill Zone*

a truly international struggle, had begun an experimental operation involving volunteers from Algeria. These young Arab Communists, led by hardcore Red officers, were to be tested against U.S. troops. If they proved effective, other nationalities would be brought in from behind the Iron Curtain to expand the insurgency against the Americans, South Vietnamese, and their allies.

Because of the possibility of failure, the Reds did not want to publicize these "volunteers" to the conflict unless the experiment proved a rousing success. The American brass also did not want the situation publicized, under any circumstances. To do so would be to play into the world-opinion manipulations of the Communists.

But the generals in Saigon wanted the situation neutralized as quickly as possible.

Thus, Falconi and the Black Eagles moved into the jungle to take on the Algerians led by fanatical Major Omar Ahmed. Ahmed, who rebelled against France in Algeria, had actually fought in the French army in Indochina as an enemy of the very people he ended up serving. Captured before the Battle of Dien Bien Phu, he had been an easy and pliable subject for the Red brainwashers and interrogators. When he returned to his native Algeria after repatriation, he was a dedicated Communist ready to take on anything the free world could throw at him.

Falconi and his men, with their communication system destroyed by deceit, fought hard. But they were badly outnumbered and finally forced into a situation where their backs were literally pinned against the wall of a jungle cliff. But Archie Dobbs, injured on the infiltration jump and evacuated from the mission back to the U.S. Army hospital at Long Binh, went AWOL in order to rejoin his buddies in combat. He not only successfully returned to them, but arrived in a helicopter gunship that threw in the fire support necessary to turn the situation around.

The Communist experiment was swept away in the volleys of aerial fire and the final bayonet charge of the Black Eagles. The end result was a promotion to lieutenant colonel for Robert Falconi while his senior noncoms also were given a boost up the army's career ladder. Only Archie Dobbs, who had gone AWOL from the hospital, was demoted.

After Operation Cambodian Challenge, the Black Eagles only received the briefest of rests back at their base garrison. This return to Camp Nui Dep with fond hopes of R&R dancing through their combat-buzzed minds was interrupted by the next challenge to their courage and ingenuity. This was a mission that was dubbed Operation Song Cai Duel.[11]

Communist patrol boats had infiltrated the Song Cai River and controlled that waterway north of Dak Bla. Their activities ranged from actual raiding of river villages and military outposts, to active operations involving the transportation and infiltration of Red agents.

This campaign resulted in the very disturbing fact that the Song Cai River, though in South Vietnam, was under the complete control of Ho Chi Minh's fighters. They virtually owned the waterway.

The brass' orders to Falconi were simple: *Get the river back!*

[11] Black Eagles No. 11—*Duel On the Song Cai*

The mission, however, was much more complicated. Distances were long, while logistics and personnel were not in the quantities needed. But that had never stopped the Black Eagles before.

There were new lessons to be learned, too. River navigation, powerboating and amphibious warfare had to be added to the Black Eagles' skills in jungle fighting.

Outgunned and outnumbered, Falconi and his guys waded in over their heads. The pressure mounted to the point that the village they used as a base headquarters had to be evacuated. But a surprise appearance by Chuck Fagin with a couple of quad-fifty machine guns turned the tide.

The final showdown was a gunboat battle that turned the muddy waters of the Song Cai red with blood.

It was pure hell for the men, but it was another brick laid in the wall of their brief and glorious history.

The next Black Eagle adventure began on a strange note. A French intelligence officer, who was a veteran of France's Indochinese War, was attached to SOG in an advisory role. While visiting the communications room, he was invited to listen in on an intermittent radio transmission in the French language that the section had been monitoring for several months. When he heard it, the Frenchman was astounded. The broadcast was from a French soldier who correctly identified himself through code as a member of the G.M.I. *(Groupement Mixte d'Intervention),* which had carried on guerrilla warfare utilizing native volunteers in the old days.[12]

Contact was made, and it was learned that this

12 Black Eagles No. 12—*Lord of Laos*

Frenchman was indeed a G.M.I. veteran who had been reported missing-in-action during mountain insurgency operations in 1953. And he'd done more than just survive for fifteen years. He was the leader of a large group of Meo tribesmen who were actively raiding into North Vietnam from Laos.

The information was kicked "upstairs" and the brass hats became excited. Not only was this man a proven ass-kicker, but he could provide valuable intelligence and an effective base of operations to launch further missions into the homeland of the Reds. It was officially decided to make contact with the man and bring him into the "Big Picture" by supplying him with arms, equipment, and money to continue his war against the Communists. The G3 Section also thought it would be a great idea to send in a detachment of troops to work with him.

They chose Lieutenant Colonel Robert Falconi and his Black Eagles for the job.

But when the detachment infiltrated the operational area they did not find a dedicated anti-Communist. Instead, they were faced with an insane French army sergeant named Farouche who reigned over an opium empire high in the Laotian mountains. He had contacted the allies only for added weaponry and money in his crazy plans to wrest power from other warlords.

The mission dissolved into sheer hell. Falconi and the guys not only had to travel by foot back through five hundred miles of enemy territory to reach the safety of friendly lines, but they had to fight both the Communists and Farouche's tribesmen every step of the way.

The effort cost them three good men, and when they finally returned to safety, Archie Dobbs found that his nurse sweetheart had left him for another man. Enraged and brokenhearted, the detachment scout took off on another escapade of AWOL, this time to track down his lady love and her new boyfriend.

Falconi also expanded his Table of Organization and built up another fire team to give the detachment a grand total of three. Ray Swift Elk was commissioned an officer and made second in command, Sergeant Major Top Gordon was released from the hospital, and Malpractice McCorckel and Calvin Culpepper returned from furlough. Six new men were added to the roster, so, despite Archie Dobbs's disappearance, the detachment was in damned good shape numerically.

But they didn't have long to sit back and enjoy their condition. Their next adventure came on them hard and fast after the Soviet Union had constructed a high-powered communications center in North Vietnam with the capability of monitoring and jamming satellite transmissions.[13] The project had been so secret that it was a long while before western intelligence heard about it. Its location was hazardous for potential attackers. There were several strong military posts in the vicinity, and the area had a heavy concentration of population.

Like they said at SOG headquarters: "Only madmen or the Black Eagles would attempt to destroy the site."

Falconi was charged with infiltrating the area, blowing up the target, then getting the hell out of there. The latter part was a big problem, and the colonel came up with a bizarre exfiltration scheme. He planned to

[13] Black Eagles 13—*Encore At Dien Bien Phu*

add insult to injury by meeting an aircraft on the reconstructed airstrip at Dien Bien Phu that had been rebuilt as a tourist site.

The Black Eagles had an asset who met them on their initial entry into the operational area. This person had been born and raised in the area and knew every nook and cranny of the terrain. The agent's identity was kept secret until the last possible moment, and Falconi's usual calm demeanor was sorely tested when he found himself working with Andrea Thuy—his former sweetheart from the detachment's "old days."

But despite emotional and tactical problems, Falconi directed a successful mission. The huge communications complex was blown to hell, and the aircraft was met for the escape after a few hectic hours of evading enemy troops.

The Black Eagle adventure that followed all this was instigated by the sensitivity and hurt feelings of a Soviet officer.[14] Lieutenant Colonel Gregori Krashchenko of the Russian KGB had been humiliated once too often by Robert Falconi and his Black Eagles. The Soviet spy's superiors agreed and gave him unlimited authority to get back at the Americans who had been kicking ass in Vietnam.

Krashchenko had very definite ideas of how to defeat an elite unit: form up a similar outfit of your own! Thus, he spent six months whipping together his own version of the Black Eagles. This group of dedicated Communists had been carefully recruited out of the ranks of the Soviet Union's most elite forces—the paratroops, naval infantry, and even specially trained scouts and trackers of the KGB

[14] Black Eagles No. 14—*Rang Dong Challenge*

Border Guard. In the spirit of international Communism, there were also some handpicked specialists from various Iron Curtain nations. This group, whom Krashchenko named the Red Bears, went through a brutally tough training program designed to whip them into shape to meet Falconi's men in the jungles of Vietnam.

Krashchenko was not fooling when he set his standards. He wanted the best and he made damned sure he got the cream of the crop. Of the one hundred and fifty men who volunteered for the Red Bears, only sixteen made the grade. These proved themselves to be the toughest of the tough as far as Communist militarism went. Dedicated to the idea of seeking out and destroying Falconi's Black Eagles, these zealots were armed with the latest weaponry and carried the best equipment. There was nothing they lacked in support from the Soviet High Command.

Completely outfitted and insane with the desire to fight, they were ready to be wound up and turned loose. The KGB notified their counterparts in the CIA of the Red Bears and threw down the gauntlet of challenge: If Falconi and his men had the balls, they'd find seventeen bad-ass Reds waiting for them in the jungle vicinity where the international borders of North Vietnam, South Vietnam, and Cambodia met.

The CIA carefully considered the dare given them. There was more at stake here than a simple test of wills and pride. The entire intelligence community of the world would be watching. The prestige—and, consequently effectiveness in recruiting and operations—of each side was part of the big pot to be won.

Thus, the challenge was accepted and Falconi took

sixteen of his hardest-hitting vets in with him for this Asian showdown where only the quick and deadly could survive.

The fighting was horrific and bloody, and did not end until the Red Bears and their crazed commander were wiped out, and eight of Falconi's men—half his command—had also given the ultimate sacrifice for their cause. They returned from the field mauled but proud, and Chuck Fagin saw to it they got a few weeks off to get their heads back together.

It is to the Black Eagles' credit that unit integrity and morale always seemed to increase despite the staggering losses they suffered. Not long after their initial inception, the detachment decided they wanted an insignia all their own. This wasn't at all unusual for units in Vietnam. Local manufacturers, acting on designs submitted to them by the troops involved, produced these emblems, which were worn by the outfits while "in country." These adornments were strictly nonregulation and unauthorized for display outside of Vietnam.

Falconi's men came up with a unique beret badge manufactured as a cloth insignia. A larger version was used as a shoulder patch. The design consisted of a black eagle—naturally—with spread wings. The big bird's beak was opened in a defiant battle cry, and he clutched a sword in one claw and a bolt of lightning in the other. Mounted on a khaki shield that was trimmed in black, the insignia was an accurate portrayal of its wearers: somber and deadly.

The Black Eagles, because of the secret nature of their existence, were not always able to sport the insignia. But when they could, the men wore it with great pride.

There was one more touch of their individuality that they kept to themselves. It was a motto, which not only worked as a damned good password in hairy situations, but also described the Black Eagles' basic philosophy.

Those special words, in Latin, were:

CALCITRA CLUNIS!

This phrase, in the language of the ancient Roman Legionnaires who served Julius Caesar, translated as: KICK ASS!

CHAPTER 4

The work session to create the OPLAN had been practically nonstop. The billets filled with cigarette and cigar smoke that floated lazily around the bare lightbulbs in the fixtures hanging from the ceiling. Ashtrays overflowed and cups of coffee steamed beside every typewriter.

Falconi had enough faith in his men's dedication to their jobs not to require that they work a set number of hours. Instead, when a man became tired and felt he really needed a rest, he climbed onto his bunk for an hour or two of sleep. Then, refreshed and feeling better, it was back to the typewriter for more work on whatever annex of the operations plan concerned that particular individual.

The one exception in getting well-deserved breaks was hard-working Gunnar Olson. As the supply sergeant, he had to tend to special chores and requests to get the equipment they needed. When word came that a specific item or packages of goods were to be drawn, the Norwegian-American sergeant had no choice but to respond quickly by going to the source to draw the supplies. He would go outside, climb wearily into the ¾-ton truck loaned to the detachment, and drive to some supply annex to pick up whatever gear he needed. The entire preparation period covered thirty hours. In that time, Gunnar managed to squeeze in a grand total of three hours of sleep, most of those rest sessions taken in increments of thirty minutes or less.

In the meantime, one by one, the annexes were presented to Falconi. He read each carefully, made notes in the margins of the documents, and gave some verbal instruction or orders on changes he wanted made in the content. There were some mild protests now and then over some minor point, but unless the writer could convince the commander to change his mind, his decision held.

Finally, the typewriters gradually grew silent and the Black Eagles finished up their paperwork. The early birds caught some extra rest by collapsing on their bunks and drifting off into fitful naps full of dreams of call signs, ammo lists, map coordinates, and other aspects of military planning.

A peaceful quietness settled over the billets in an atmosphere of serene tranquility.

"Awright! Off your asses!" Sergeant Major Top Gordon bellowed. "What the fuck do you think this is?

Nappy time in a kindergarten? There's a briefing to conduct here. Move! Move! Move!"

There was a stampede of feet to punctuate the choruses of curses as the men leaped from the bunks and shoved their way into the briefing area. Falconi stood at the front of the room and waited as his troops settled into the metal folding chairs that had been arranged there for them.

Top Gordon stepped forward. "De-tachment, tinch-hut!"

Every man-jack leaped to his feet and snapped to the position of attention.

"Sir," Top said. "The detachment is all present and accounted for. Ready for briefing."

Falconi returned his salute. "Thank you, sergeant major." He motioned to the men. "Take your seats. Smoke if you have them."

The men settled back to learn the complete story behind this new mission that had been assigned to their unit.

"This little adventure we're going on has been titled Operation Hellhound by the brass at SOG," Falconi said. "The name doesn't mean much to you, but the mission does. We have been instructed to interdict and destroy Viet Cong infiltration and supply delivery trails in the western operational areas." He turned to a map pinned on the wall behind him. "You'll find the O.A. at coordinates 10822512359—" He paused as the men consulted their personal copies of the maps issued them with the OPLANs. "That is the exact center of the area, so it is not difficult to conclude we'll be shittin' and gittin' 360 degrees around that particular point.

55

That's about it in nice, straightforward, simple terms. Now I'll turn the floor over to Swift Elk, who will give you the much more complicated concept of the operation."

Ray Swift Elk strode to the front of the room. He turned and faced the men, his dark countenance serious. "Our entry into the operational area will be by a method that we've never used before. And there is no doubt in my mind that it's going to be one of the hairiest. Our previous modes of going into the hot zones has been by parachute mostly, and we've done a couple of water infiltrations that have included submarines and rivercraft."

Archie Dobbs laughed. "You sound real mysterious, sir."

Swift Elk smiled at him. "Okay. Then I'll ease the suspenseful atmosphere. We'll be using a technique known in the military trade as 'Stay Behind.'"

"Stay behind?" Calvin Culpepper said. "How about pissing on this operation and 'staying behind' in the Saigon bars?"

"No way, Buffalo Soldier," Swift Elk said. "Stay Behind, in this instance, means going into the area with another unit to engage the enemy. When the outfit moves out we'll—"

"—stay behind!" Paulo Garcia said, completing the sentence.

"Right," Swift Elk said. "There is an ARVN ranger battalion that has been using armored personnel carriers for deep penetration hit-and-run operations. We'll go in with them, then fade out into the jungle prior to their withdrawal."

Buffalo Soldier Culpepper nodded his head in understanding. "Then when things get quiet, we'll liven 'em up again."

"Correct," Swift Elk said. "We're scheduled to remain out there for a long time. Up to four, even five months, if that turns out to be necessary. We are ordered to do whatever nasty things we can dream up to spoil the travels of the Viet Cong into South Vietnam. We'll do a lot of living off the land, between parachute supply drops and stealing from the enemy. That means we'll be conducting guerrilla warfare in its purest form, except we won't have any local support."

Blue Richard bit off a chaw of Red Chief chewing tobacco. "That means guerrilla versus guerrilla."

"That means pure hell!" Archie Dobbs said.

"Give the man a cigar," Swift Elk said. "That's it for any discussion on the concept, guys. You should fully understand what the big shots want us to do, so I'll let Sergeant Major Gordon cover the execution phase."

"Thank you, sir," Top said, taking over the briefing. "Listen up! Tomorrow's reveille is tonight, at 2000 hours."

There was a collective groan from the men.

"Hey," Top said. "Who told you jokers to join the service for sleep, anyhow? We're canceling tonight and starting tomorrow today, that's all. We'll board trucks at 2215, which means you'll be packed and ready to roll before you turn in, and we'll join the ranger unit out in the field at 0500 hours. Their penetration into enemy territory is set for 0700 hours, and it's estimated that we should be in our stay-behind position by noon."

Archie checked his map. "What's the coordinates of

57

that place we'll be hiding, sergeant major?"

"We can't forecast that, Archie," Top said. "That's because there is no way to know how the battle will go. If our ARVN pals enjoy a lot of success, we can pick and choose the spot. If they start getting their asses kicked, then we'll have to make do with whatever the situation offers. But no matter what happens, we'll stay behind and lay low and be nice and quiet until late afternoon to convince any VC in the vicinity that the area is empty. Then we'll send out a couple of recon patrols to check things out and find a base camp. We'll begin kicking ass ASAP after that. Questions? Good. Now I'll let Paulo give the intelligence and communications briefing."

Staff Sergeant Paulo Garcia of the U.S. Marine Corps took a sheaf of notes with him. He shuffled through them and selected one. "Okay. Let's talk commo. In that particular area, we'll be following the good old KISS principle—Keep It Simple, Stupid. There will be four Prick-Six radios for talking amongst ourselves. Colonel Falconi will have one, and his call sign will be 'Falcon.' Lieutenant Swift Elk will be 'Horse,' Sergeant Major Gordon will be 'Kicker,' and Archie Dobbs will be 'Nosey.'"

"Nosey?" Archie protested, jumping to his feet. "What kind o' stupid fucking call sign is that?"

Top Gordon glared at him. "I thought it up."

"And it's a real good one too, sergeant major!" Archie exclaimed, sitting back down.

Paulo grinned. "Any more comments, Archie?"

"Nope."

"Okay," Paulo said, continuing. "I'll tote the big set

58

and will be making contacts with the forward stations on the SOG net. Our call sign will be 'Eagle.' So if I buy the farm, I want the next guy to man that radio to know that."

"There there communications talk is real inter'sting," Buffalo Soldier Culpepper said. "But tell us about the bad guys, Paulo."

"Okay," Paulo said. "Here's the word on the opposition. These are veteran Viet Cong troops working in company and battalion strength as security and transportation to keep infiltration trails open that are used to bring men, ammo, and supplies to fight against South Vietnam."

Ray Swift Elk raised his hand. "Are these all part of one big unit, Paulo?"

"No, sir," Paulo answered. "They're independent units, but they are directed by an area command rather than a brigade or division headquarters."

"If we find the brains of the operation," Archie mused, "then we could put a real crimp in their style by wiping out the bastards."

"What really pisses me off," Paulo continued, "is that the sonofabitches think they can waltz into their operational areas as they damned well please. They even have rest areas for their worn-out troops to recuperate in."

"Let's give 'em reason to have some graveyards to relax in," Archie said ominously. "How many of them bastards are there supposed to be there, Paulo?"

"We're not sure of the enemy's numerical strength in the area," Paulo said. "But G2 has estimated there are probably a thousand or so Viet Cong involved in these activities." He paused and smiled. "That means there's probably three times that many."

Blue shifted the chaw in his mouth. "Let's see—" he stood up and counted, "—they's nine of us, so that means we'll be outnumbered considerable. There oughta be 'bout three hunnerd plus o' them damn VC for each one of us. That might make for some inter'sting shooting."

"Yeah," Buffalo Soldier Culpepper agreed. *"Both* ways."

"Some of the VC are what they call 'joy-girls.' Those are camp prostitutes, to give the boys some real relaxation after a hard campaign," Paulo said.

Blue leered. "I wonder where I can borry me a loan on some black pajamas so's I could line up for some o' that."

Top Gordon laughed. "We're supposed to search and destroy, Blue. Not search and infiltrate."

"I'll bet Blue was thinking of some special infiltration," Archie said, winking at his friend.

"Okay, Big Team," Paulo said. "That's the word on commo and the bad guys. I'll turn the stage over to Buffalo Soldier for the word on demo and engineering."

Buffalo Soldier Calvin Culpepper took the floor. "Our initial demolitions is gonna be Claymore mines," he said. "If we need anything else, like maybe C-4, we'll have Gunnar call it in for us. There's always the outside chance we'll have to blow a pontoon bridge or plank road. Whatever it is, me and Blue will handle it. We ain't sure if there's any enemy vehicles involved that would mean extensive mining operations. Right now, I'm forecasting plenty o' antipersonnel work in that

60

particular line o' warfare. That's it from me and Blue's side o' the house. Now I'll call on my good friend Gunnar to entertain us all with his rendition of the supply annex of the operations plan. Gunnar, get on down!"

Gunnar showed no tendency to be jovial. He was too damned tired. He spoke in a monotone as he referred to his notes. "We'll take in M16s and hand grenades, along with pistols," he said. "If we feel the need for anything heavier, we'll request it in a supply drop. That goes for rations, special equipment, and replacement stuff, too."

"Gunnar," Top Gordon said. "How often can we expect to have supply drops?"

Gunnar shrugged. "Never regular and not real often," he answered. "We'll be doing a lot of living off the land and stealing from the Viet Cong, like the colonel said, so pull in your belts a notch or two. There may be some hungry days out there." He sighed. "I hate to say it, guys, but from the way things look, I figure we'll be toting AK47s and shooting 7.62 millimeter bullets before all is said and done on this thing. Our best source of supply is gonna be Uncle Ho up in North Vietnam. That's it in a nutshell. I'll let Malpractice give you the medical briefing now."

Malpractice didn't bother to go to the front. "The first thing I want you to do is—"

Everyone sang out, "—use your water purification tablets!"

Malpractice frowned. "Go ahead and make fun, you stupid bastards. But the first dumbass that comes to me with diarrhea from drinking brackish water is gonna

61

get a hell of a lot more than some pills. Also, tend to cuts and scratches out there, infection in the jungle comes easy, and it kills."

"What's the word on medevac?" Paulo asked.

"We'll get a wounded man out," Malpractice promised. "But it's probably going to take some time."

"Hey, Malpractice!" Archie called. "What if a tiger bites my arm off? Have you got a pill for that?"

Malpractice shook his head. "Archie, there ain't a thing devised by medical science that could save that poor tiger." He sneered at Archie. "Now if there's no more stupid comments, I'll turn you stupid shits back over to the sergeant major."

Top Gordon marched to the front of the room. "Detachment, tinch-hut!"

They stood up rigid and military as Lieutenant Colonel Robert Falconi went to the front of the room.

Top saluted. "Sir, the detachment is briefed."

"Thank you, sergeant major." Falconi turned and faced his men. "At ease and take your seats." He waited for them to settle down. "Men, we're cut back now until we're lean and mean. The job that's been handed down to us is tailor-made for a detachment like this. But it's a long, dirty one that's going to get a hell of a lot worse before it gets better. I don't have to emphasize the danger, and I don't have to emphasize why this assignment has been given us. It's not because we're good, goddamn it, it's because we're the best!"

There was a spontaneous cheer from the men.

"We won a great victory last time out into the cold," Falconi went on, "and we paid a terrible price for it. Despite heavy losses, the brass has called on us again.

They're doing it because they need us. That means your country needs you, too. So, do your jobs, cover your asses and your buddies' asses, and kick the VC's asses—*calcitra clunis.*"

"Amen," Buffalo Soldier Culpepper said. "Some o' God's chillun are going to war."

CHAPTER 5

The convoy crawled through the dense, hot tropical night. Despite being in the open back of a deuce-and-half truck, the Black Eagles perspired heavily in the steamy weather. They had boarded the vehicle five hours earlier at Peterson Field. After a quick trip to Long Binh to join other trucks in a large convoy, the detachment began a sluggish ride toward their destination, where they were to link up with the South Vietnamese ranger outfit.

Despite the slowness of the journey, no one complained. The security for the long caravan of trucks was complete as it moved out of Saigon and into the open country beyond. Roving patrols of jeeps moved up and down the line, and there were plenty of stops while suspicious circumstances were checked out by men who dismounted from their vehicles and crept into the dark woods beyond to search for potential ambushers. In fact, the very timing of this convoy—night—was a surprise move. Traveling through the darkness on roads in VC territory was so dangerous that the Communist guerrillas had never considered that anyone would try it. So they had never set out ambushes for that particular time.

That meant, of course, that for many months to come the Red guerrillas would be prepared for nocturnal travelers, until they once again felt it wasn't worth the effort.

This convoy was a purely American organization out of South Vietnam's capital city. Its mission was the delivery of supplies and personnel to areas toward the fighting, and the man in charge of its safety—a bull-voiced Military Police captain—was damned good at his job. And he wouldn't let anyone, despite rank or position, push him into moving faster.

The Black Eagles either dozed on the floor of the truck bed, or sat up and let what breeze was available blow across them. They became restless at times, yet as combat veterans they knew the value of getting as much sleep as possible whenever the opportunity was open to them.

So they mostly slept.

Toward dawn, when the pinkish light in the east foretold the rising sun, the trucks picked up some speed. But just as it looked like they might go all the way to 30 mph, the convoy suddenly came to a halt.

Falconi, in the cab, climbed down to the roadway and went forward. He saw the MP captain talking to a

South Vietnamese army officer. Both saluted as the colonel walked up. The Vietnamese smiled. "You are Colonel Falconi?"

"Yes," Falconi answered. "Would you be Major Ngoyen?"

"Yes. My ranger battalion is on the other side of that tree line, colonel. We anxiously await your arrival."

"Fine," Falconi said. He turned to the MP officer. "This is where we leave you, captain. I appreciate the fine way you've run this convoy. Particularly the idea of starting the thing in the black of night."

The captain shrugged. "It worked this time, but it won't so easy again. At least not for a few weeks. Then I'll run me another one." He displayed a slight smile. "I hope the plan pays off that time, too."

Falconi winked at him. "But you can bet some VC commander is going to get his ass chewed about it. That means a few of his men will be going without sleep while manning ambushes that will never happen. You're a sharp man."

The MP laughed. "The closer the enemy, the more efficient the officer, right, sir?"

"Absolutely," Falconi agreed. He turned to the truck. "Sergeant major!"

"Yes, sir?"

"Let's un-ass the vehicle," Falconi said.

Gordon saw to it that the men quickly got their gear and leaped down to the roadway and formed up off to one side. They stayed there long enough for the long line of trucks to pull away and move on down the two-lane macadam highway.

Major Ngoyen was not a man to stand on ceremony. "Please to follow me with your men, Colonel Falconi."

67

He looked at his watch. "We will launch our operation within fifteen minutes."

Falconi, now wearing his own field gear, looked back to notice his men had struggled into their own equipment. "Well, guys, let's not keep the major and his battalion waiting."

The Black Eagles, in a single file, moved off the road and trailed after the two officers into the jungle. After crossing through a shallow treeline, they stepped into a wide-open area where dozens of armored personnel carriers were parked. The superb discipline of the Vietnamese was evident in that there had not been one sound to give them away. These troops, well-trained and tough, sat silently in their heavy conveyances.

Major Ngoyen indicated an empty one. "That is for you and your men, colonel. We will move forward until we engage the enemy."

Falconi glanced around. "How far away are they? We're very close to the road."

Ngoyen smiled. "The Viet Cong own all this country around here, Colonel Falconi. Except where my brave men and I decide to go. We will be able to drive in any direction and make contact."

"Jesus!" Falconi said. "Our brass weren't kidding when they said this territory was a busy infiltration point for the Reds."

"Indeed," Ngoyen agreed. "If I had enough men, I could kick them out. But—" he shrugged, "I can only hit them one place at a time. As soon as I leave, they come in and pick up their dead and carry on."

"Perhaps my unit and I can change that a bit," Falconi said.

"You are brave to stay out here," Ngoyen said. "And

I wish you very good luck."

"Thank you," Falconi said. He turned to the detachment and pointed at the APC. "Well, guys, get in. It's time to get this show on the road."

The men crowded into the enclosed conveyance and arranged their rucksacks and other equipment in the center as they settled down on the long benches that ran the length of each side.

There were two Vietnamese rangers already aboard. One manned the .50 caliber heavy machine gun at the front, and the other was the driver. The gunner waved at the Americans, then turned his attention back to his weapon.

The driver displayed a gap-toothed grin. "Hello, Joe!"

Archie Dobbs was sitting the closest to him. "How're you doing, pal?"

"Hello, Joe!"

Archie laughed. "The name is Archie. What's your handle?"

"Hello, Joe!" the Vietnamese repeated.

"Hey, ol' buddy," Blue Richards called out to him. "How fast does this here armored personnel carrier go?"

"Hello, Joe!"

Archie frowned. "I think that's the only English he knows."

Blue leaned across the scout to speak closer to the ranger. "Do you speak English?"

"Hello, Joe!" Then the ARVN soldier displayed the only other words he knew in the American's language. "Where is the post office?"

Archie laughed and slapped the guy's shoulder.

69

"Hello, Joe!"

The Vietnamese was delighted he'd finally established rapport with his passengers. "Hello, Joe!" But before he could repeat himself, there was a shouted order in Vietnamese from outside. The man immediately became serious and punched the starter button.

The big engine kicked to life and its roar drowned out any further attempts at conversation. The gunner pulled a headset and microphone from a canvas bag mounted on the bulkhead. After plugging the commo equipment into a jack on the dash, he handed it over to Falconi.

The colonel had just put on the gear when he heard a voice come over the air. "Falcon, this is Ran. Over."

Falconi recognized Major Ngoyen's voice using the Vietnamese word for "snake" as a call sign. "Ran, this is Falcon. Over."

"Falcon, stay buttoned down until I give you the word to leave the APC. Your driver is instructed on what he must do. Tap him hard on the back, and he will lower the rear ramp. Over."

"Roger, Ran. Out."

The APC lurched forward to begin a noisy, hot, dusty ride full of bumps and turns that made the human cargo inside lurch from side to side with the violent maneuvers of the vehicle.

The uncomfortable ride went on for more than an hour. The angry curses of the Black Eagles went unheard over the thundering racket of the engine. But their scowls and red faces showed the anger that was building up in them. Gunnar Olson, at one point, made a lunge for the driver in an impulsive desire to beat the hell out of him, but cooler heads prevailed as Paulo

70

Garcia and Buffalo Soldier Culpepper grabbed him and prevented an international incident.

Then the shooting started.

The gunner, standing up at his position with his head above a circular opening, fired his weapon in controlled pulls on the trigger. The reports of the heavy machine gun could barely be heard, but the expended brass could easily be seen bouncing off the steel deck of the APC.

Each Black Eagle instinctively grabbed his M16 rifle and locked and loaded a full thirty-round magazine. Now their conveyance was really whipping around as whatever fighting was going on outside began to grow in intensity. A couple of heavy pings on the side showed they'd been hit, but the metal hull of the APC warded off whatever had been fired on them.

Then they could see the gunner's legs suddenly straighten up. The soldier abruptly collapsed to the deck. A massive head wound showed where the fatal shot had hit him. Gunnar the Gunner leaped forward again, this time too quick to be stopped. He pulled the ranger's body aside and took over the machine gun position. Now, with his head and upper torso in the turret, he could see the maneuvering of the other armored personnel carriers. Gunnar quickly spotted the enemy positions they were charging. The Minnesota lad sent out fusillades of heavy automatic fire while his detachment mates watched and silently wished him luck.

Another fifteen minutes of the wildly gyrating battle went on. Once again the earphones crackled and Falconi could hear Major Ngoyen's voice. "Falcon, this is Ran. Over."

71

"This is Falcon. Over."

"It is time for you to leave us. You will find good cover to the left of your vehicle. I know you will do well on your campaign. *Chao ong. Thurong-lo binh-an!* Over."

"Thank you," Falconi said. "Good-bye and good luck to you, too. Out." He took off the headset and threw it to the floor. After pulling on Gunnar's pant leg to signal him to leave the machine gun, Falconi slapped the driver on the back.

The armored personnel carrier slammed to such a quick halt that everyone fell forward. By the time they recovered, the ramp was down.

"Let's go!" Falconi ordered. He grabbed his rucksack and raced out of the vehicle to the outside. The rest of the detachment followed as he led them to the left. There was a dense stand of trees there. Falconi's idea was to get inside the heavy vegetation and lay low.

The Viet Cong already there had other ideas.

The incoming fire swept through the detachment. They quickly formed up in a skirmish line under Falconi's shouted orders. "Paulo! Blue! You're automatic riflemen!"

The two Black Eagles switched the selectors on their M16 rifles to full automatic and began hosing forward. Their unit mates, struggling along clumsily in their heavy gear, kept up a steady staccato of individual shots.

A couple of the more careless black-pajama-clad VC were hit. They jerked violently from the impact of the volley, falling into twisted heaps.

Top Gordon took time for a steady, but quick sight picture on another Red. He squeezed the trigger and was satisfied to note the man staggering backward under the blow of the bullet before collapsing. But he was not satisfied with the alignment of the attack formation. "Archie! Slow it down! Malpractice, step out!"

The enemy in the trees was a rifle squad armed with AK47s. They used their weaponry to its best advantage, but the unexpected dismounted assault had caught them completely by surprise. Although they fought hard, their defense melted away as the cross fire from the enveloping Black Eagle detachment wrapped around them like the tentacles of an octopus.

When Falconi's men entered the position, the lieutenant colonel quickly ordered them to cease fire. "We've got to get these bodies out of here!" he shouted over the roar of the battle around them. "When Ngoyen's APCs pull out, the Charlies are going to come back to retrieve their dead."

The men immediately began picking up the corpses and carrying them out from the cover of the trees to deposit them a few dozen meters away.

"Goddamnit!" Top Gordon cursed. "Don't lay the sonofabitches out so neat. Make 'em look like they were shot dead and fell there."

"How's this, sergeant major?" Archie asked. He picked one dead man up by the arm pits and struggled until he had the guy in a standing position. Then he let him drop.

"Push him away from you," Malpractice, the medical expert, said. "That'll make it look like he was knocked over from the force of the bullet."

Archie tried again. "What do think?"

"Now that," Top said, "looks like a man who died

73

proudly for Communism."

Within ten minutes, the massacred squad was arranged to look like they'd gone down in the open. The Black Eagles positioned themselves in the cover of the trees and waited.

After a half hour the shooting stopped. Within another ten minutes, the South Vietnam armored personnel carriers came back into view and swept past them on the way back to the ARVN's original attack position.

Then silence.

Falconi took a deep breath and slowly exhaled. "This, gentlemen," he said softly, "is where the shit hits the fan."

74

CHAPTER 6

The Black Eagles lay quietly under the cover of the dense jungle vegetation for more than an hour. The heat, heavy and persistent, was smothering. The men could taste the salt on their lips as perspiration trickled down from their boonie hats in heavy rivulets.

The silence, which was nearly as oppressive as the temperature and humidity, was broken when Archie's ominous whisper sounded from his position in the perimeter of the trees: "They're coming!"

Three VC point men appeared first.

With AK47s at the ready, they cautiously checked out the area before the appearance of the main body of Reds. The bores of their AK47s swung ominously back and forth as the guerrillas covered areas of possible attack. Finally, when they were satisfied things were safe and under control, they signaled back to their comrades. The others stepped out into the clearing from the surrounding jungle. There seemed to be so many that Falconi and his men seriously wondered if every Charlie in South Vietnam was present and accounted for right there in front of them.

It didn't take long for the Communist commander to issue orders to his men and organize their tasks. A few fanned out and set up a perimeter of defense. Others began the grim job of policing up their dead.

Archie Dobbs, who could see much more than the rest of the detachment, noted that the VC had all gone into battle with short lengths of rope tied around their ankles. The reason behind this became clear when the living grasped these nylon cords, using them to pull the corpses to a central area. Others, waiting for the dead, lifted up the deceased fighters for Ho Chi Minh and dumped them onto wheelbarrow devices to be trundled out of the immediate vicinity for burial.

Blue Richards, as usual, had positioned himself up a tree. From his vantage point, he could see that the men picking up the bodies were part of a much larger group. As each cartload of three VC dead was rolled away from the battle site, it was passed on to waiting hands that moved the crude vehicles and their morbid loads farther into the jungle.

The Alabamian made a mental note of what was happening. The activity obviously meant there was either a trail or some cleared assembly point nearby. He smiled to himself when he considered the opportunities for ambush that such a situation offered. It would be even easier than shooting treed raccoons back home in Barbour County.

Down on the ground, and about twenty meters from Blue, another Black Eagle lay in concealment. Paulo Garcia, well camouflaged under a dense bush that grew between two tall trees, couldn't see much. His vision was severely limited to a space between ground level and about two feet above that. Thick leaves and other foliage prevented a better view. Now and then he could see the black pajama legs and sandals of nearby VC as they scurried past him. There was also the rather disturbing sight of mangled human wreckage that was pulled across his limited field of vision. Paulo barely breathed while the enemy probed the area for dead and wounded. As he continued his silent observation, he was relatively unconcerned, until a rather serious realization finally popped into his mind:

The VC were drawing closer and closer to his position.

They were making efficient, deliberate sweeps back and forth in their search for their casualties. These superbly disciplined jungle fighters barely said a word to each other as they examined places to which a dying or badly injured guerrilla might crawl in the heat of battle.

Now and then there would be a whispered exclamation. Paulo could see a physical investigation made that always resulted in a dead Charlie being dragged by that ankle rope from beneath some cover. This probing continued for another half hour—until they were finally at Paulo's own private bush.

A bamboo stick was thrust into the leaves as a probe

77

for a human form. Paulo gritted his teeth and was barely able to dodge the device as it bounced up and down around him several times. He quietly eased himself away, then was immediately forced to grit his teeth from crying out in pain.

A VC was standing on his hand!

The fellow had stepped in closer to the branches and leaves in his attempt to locate any potential cadavers. What he didn't realize was that the only creature nearby was living and breathing—and getting pissed off. The weight of the foot increased and Paulo felt sharp stabs of pain from his wrist down to his fingertips.

Discovery seemed only moments away. With his desperate mind racing wildly, the Black Eagle formed a wild plan of leaping up and blasting into the VC crowd. Then he would break for freedom, running like hell to draw the Charlies away from his fellow detachment members.

But the Red guerrilla quickly finished his search and moved, lifting the weight of his foot off Paulo. The VC began slowly to work his way farther toward his buddies. Paulo pulled his throbbing fist protectively to his chest.

After another quarter of an hour passed, the VC commander issued some terse orders and the entire group formed up. A quick head count was made to make sure none of these dedicated soldiers of world socialism had deserted. After this roll call, they melted away with the same speed and grace with which they had first appeared.

Blue slid down from the tree. He met Archie who was

coming in from farther out. Archie winked at him. "Hey, Blue. Could you see much from up there?"

Blue nodded. "You bet! C'mon. I figger there's a hell of a lot more around here than can be seen. Let's find the Falcon."

While the pair sought out their commanding officer, the other members of the detachment stationed themselves at various points that offered the best fields of fire in case the VC withdrawal was a feint. This was done under Top Gordon's less than gentle direction.

Falconi and Lieutenant Ray Swift Elk were studying a map when Archie and Blue found them. "Sir," Blue announced, "they's a trail on over to the west there."

Ray Swift Elk was interested. "Are you sure?"

"Yes, sir," Blue answered. "I seen them Charlies hauling their stiffs on them wheelbarrow doo-dads over to the area and wheeling them away."

Falconi was pleased with the news. "It looks like the first day is going to begin with a success. Our orders are to disrupt their supply routes, and it looks like we can get started real early on that particular job."

"Show us where the thing runs on the map, Blue," Swift Elk said.

"Right here, sir," Blue said. "At first I couldn't see nothin'. But after a while, I finally made out where them rascals was a-goin'." Like all Navy Seals, he was an expert in topography and map reading. "It starts at about that there contour line and goes straight west. From where I was a-hanging in that tree, it looked like it turned south."

Falconi lit a cigarette. "That could be the location of

79

an important junction."

"I better check it out, sir," Archie said.

"Right," Falconi said. "And take Blue with you. He can watch your back while you're sneaking and peeking out there."

"Aye, aye, sir," Blue responded.

"Let's go," Archie said, tugging on him.

"Shithouse mouse! I'm waiting on *you!*" Blue said in protest at being pulled along.

At the moment the two left on their patrol, Paulo Garcia showed up at the impromptu command post. He looked around. "Where's Malpractice?"

Swift Elk pointed to a grove of bamboo. "Through there." He noticed the marine sergeant was holding his hand. "Did you get hurt?"

Paulo shook his head. "Nothing to write home about, sir. It's just that the fucking VC used my mitt for a parade ground." He went into the bamboo and walked past Calvin Culpepper and Gunnar Olson before he finally found the detachment medic. He squatted down beside Malpractice. "I got my hand messed up a little," he explained, holding it out.

Malpractice instantly adopted his best bedside manner. "What happened?" he asked, giving the injured member a cursory first examination.

"One o' them VC walked on it," Paulo said. He licked his lips. "It's kinda sensitive."

"Yeah?" Malpractice gingerly felt the hand. "Does that hurt?"

"A little bit," Paulo said in understatement.

"Move your fingers," Malpractice said.

Paulo tried. "I can only move one."

80

Malpractice noted it was the trigger finger. He held out his own hand. "Grab ahold and squeeze."

Paul strained so hard that he grimaced with the effort, but could only accomplish a weak grasp. "Shit!"

"It's broke," Malpractice said. "I don't need an x-ray to tell me that." He stood up. "C'mon. We're gonna talk to the Falcon about a medevac."

"Bullshit!" Paulo exclaimed, looking up at him. "I sure as hell ain't going no place, Malpractice. You put a splint or something on it, hear?"

Malpractice reached down and grabbed Paulo by his patrol harness. "I know what's best for you." He roughly hauled Paulo to his feet. "So don't argue with my professional medical decisions or I'll break your nose."

Paulo frowned. "You know something, man? You're really weird!"

"It don't matter," Malpractice said. "Let's go see the Falcon."

They found their commanding officer still deep in a map conference with Ray Swift Elk. Falconi sensed something was wrong by the expression on his medical sergeant's face. "What's up?"

"Paulo's got a fractured hand," Malpractice said. "I think he should be medevacked as soon as possible."

"Well, I don't!" Paulo protested. "Looky, sir. My trigger finger still works." He wiggled the digit.

Ray Swift Elk was a practical commissioned officer. "Give us a demonstration of your firing technique, Paulo."

"Okay, sir." He brought the M16 up and simulated firing. It was a little clumsy. "Well, hell! I ain't gonna

81

score expert on the range, but I can sure as hell be a good automatic rifleman."

Falconi agreed. "What can you do for his hand, Malpractice?"

"I can splint it in a way to leave the finger working," Malpractice said. "But if them bones knit crooked, he'll have a hell of a convalescence." He gently took Paulo's hand and studied it. "The sawbones is gonna have to break it again. It could take three, maybe four operations to put it right."

"Okay," Falconi said, shifting his gaze back to the marine. "It's up to you. What'll it be?"

"I'm staying, sir," Paulo said.

"Okay, tough guy," Malpractice said. "Let's get back to my medical kit and splint that mother up."

They disappeared back into the bamboo grove. Falconi looked over at Swift Elk. "The guy has an honorable way out of a dangerous situation. Nobody would argue with the idea of him going back. But he insists on hanging in there. What do you do with troops like that?"

"Fight wars, sir," Swift Elk said, turning his attention back to the map.

As the two Black Eagle officers continued their impromptu staff meeting, Archie Dobbs and Blue Richards moved through the jungle until they finally reached the trail that the Navy Seal had seen from the tree.

"Damn!" Archie whispeed. "This is a well-traveled piece of real estate, all right. It even looks like somebody goes to a lot o' trouble to take care of it."

"No shit," Blue agreed. "And that baby must be

twelve feet wide."

"Yeah," Archie said. "You ain't gonna drive no trucks on it, but two of them special bicycles for wheeling supplies could pass each other without any problems." He spent a couple of minutes listening to see if there was any nearby activity that might prove both dangerous and unfriendly. But all he could perceive were the regular sounds of the jungle. "Let's go take a look-see."

"Right," Blue said. "I'll cover your ass."

It was impossible to utilize the thick brush alongside the track. Not only would it have been too noisy and slow, but the two Black Eagles would not have been able to see anything, or anyone, until they had literally stumbled onto them.

The only alternative—and that wasn't much better— was to walk slowly up the wide supply path and hope like hell that no wandering Charlies would come charging down from the opposite direction.

Archie concentrated on studying the impressions left by humans and their implements on the trail. Bicycle tire tracks and countless rubber-soled sandals had made marks that were constantly obliterated by others of the same kind. Since the year was well into the dry season, the ground was hard-packed and solid.

Blue watched the trail ahead for any interlopers. He also swung his eyes up into the trees to check for observers posted there. But the VC clearly considered the area supersafe. They had taken no special pains to post guards. Blue and Archie continued on until it was obvious some sort of activity was approaching them.

"Archie!" Blue whispered. "Strangers a-coming!"

Both silently entered the thick vegetation off to the side. Within a few moments a squad of VC infantry, their weapons carelessly slung over their shoulders, sauntered past in an informal, casual formation. Archie gave them enough time to get well out of the immediate area. He nudged Blue. "What do you think?"

"I think we oughta hotfoot it back to the Falcon and get some shit going," Blue said. "These here Charlies is just asking for our attention."

The two went more slowly back down the track. They wanted no unpleasant surprises, in case the Charlies stopped for a break or suddenly decided to turn around and come back. But all was well, and they reached the point where they'd stepped out onto the trail without incident. After another look around, Archie and Blue reentered the jungle for the return to their detachment.

A half hour later, Falconi had received the full report. Archie not only pointed out the exact lay of the VC supply track, he took a ballpoint pen and drew it accurately on the commander's map. "There's that bend me and Blue found."

Falconi lit a cigarette. "That's where we'll pull an ambush."

Swift Elk agreed. "And there's ample area for a quick withdrawal, in case we find out something unpleasant has taken place."

Blue frowned in minor worry. "What do you think might happen?"

"Well," Swift Elk mused. "Maybe the entire Soviet Army will arrive to join their VC buddies in this war."

"If they have," Falconi said dryly, "this will be our first and last ambush of this operation." He took a drag of the cigarette. "I really have to give these things up."

"Yeah," Swift Elk said. "They're certainly hazardous to your health." Then he winked. "Like botched ambushes."

CHAPTER 7

Sergeant Major Top Gordon took off his boonie hat and wiped his nearly bald head with his olive-drab neckerchief. "C'mon! C'mon!" he said irritably. The detachment walked past him in single file, each man being assigned to a specific area by the top kick as he appeared out of the brush.

"Calvin, go to the head of the position."

"Right, sergeant major," the Buffalo Soldier said. Then he added the vow uttered by the French soldiers at the Battle of Verdun in World War I. "They shall not pass!"

"Knock off the shit and move out," Top said. "Here we are setting up an ambush and you act like we're organizing a garden party, for Chrissake!" He gestured to Malpractice. "Stick with the Buffalo Soldier. You and him has got to keep the cap on this thing."

"Clear, sergeant major!"

"That's what I like," Top said. "A businesslike attitude." He waited for the next man. "Gunnar," he said as the Norwegian-American came abreast of him.

"Yeah, Top?"

"Stay with me. We'll be between the close-up team and the officers."

"Right," Gunnar said. He stopped and stood alongside the sergeant major. "I just wish I had me a machine gun."

"Well," Top considered. "Maybe you'll get your hands on an NVA one before all is said and done around here."

"I sure as hell hope so," Gunnar said, a tone of complaint in his voice.

Paulo Garcia, sporting the splint on his injured hand, showed up and wordlessly waited for his assignment. Top pointed a few meters away. "Situate yourself over there. You'll be between us and the officers. That puts you in the middle. Since you're the automatic rifleman, you can be ready there to support anybody who needs it."

"Right, Top," Paulo said, hurrying away.

Lieutenant Colonel Robert Falconi and First Lieutenant Ray Swift Elk were the final ones to make an appearance. They stopped and Falconi lit a cigarette. "I really have to give these things up," he said, exhaling. "And that's no shit."

"Yes, sir," Top, a devoted cigar smoker, replied dully.

"Is everybody in position, Top?" Swift Elk asked.

"Yes, sir. This is where me and Gunnar the Gunner are gonna stay. Once you and the Falcon are up farther we'll be ready," Top said.

"What about Blue and Archie?" Falconi inquired.

"They got to pick their own spots," Top said. He looked at his watch. "They've had plenty of time to get ready."

"If those guys make a mistake, we're in for a hell of a miserable afternoon," Falconi said.

"Yes, sir," the sergeant major replied. "But keep in mind that if they screw up, we won't live through the whole afternoon. So the misery won't last long."

"Now that's a cheerful thought," Falconi said. He took a drag from the cigarette, then looked at it. "I'm not kidding. I'm going to give these up."

"Yes, sir," Top said, unconvinced. He looked at his watch. As the top sergeant, his job in ambush situations gave him authority over even the officers. He exercised the rights of his office without ceremony. "You and Lieutenant Swift Elk better get in position."

Falconi sighed. "Now comes the 'hurry up and wait' part of it."

"Yes, sir," Top said. "That's worse than the fighting, ain't it?"

"It sure is," Falconi said. He field-stripped the cigarette and scattered the ashes around after rolling up the paper into a little ball and flipping it away. "Come on, Ray. Know any good Indian war stories?"

"As a matter of fact I do," Swift Elk said. "Once my grandpa told me about the time when his own grandpa was in a war party ran into a cavalry patrol out of Fort—"

The two officers' voices faded away as they went to

their positions. Gunnar wordlessly chose a firing site and began the brief task of preparing it with camouflage. Top did the same. The sergeant major gave his partner a long look. Finally he asked, "How're you doing, Gunnar?"

"Okay," Gunnar said, arranging a bush to his liking. "I got me a real good view here."

"I don't mean in preparing your firing point there. I'm talking about your life in general." Top had been worried about the young soldier since the last mission. The loss of his good friend Tiny Burke had been a terrible blow, but the Scandinavian had displayed little grief. When Gunnar didn't answer him straight out, the sergeant major tried a different approach. "Gunnar, is there anything you want to talk about?"

"Nope."

"Well," Top said pulling his machete from its scabbard to begin his own chore of camouflaging. "If there ever is, just look me up."

"Okay."

Within a very short time, both were positioned and ready.

Falconi's plan for the ambush was simple but deadly in its potential effectiveness. The detachment arranged themselves on one side of the trail where it made a lazy curve through the jungle. The Black Eagle commander reasoned that this would be a place where any potential victims would instinctively slow down. The far end of the ambush, manned by Buffalo Soldier Culpepper and Malpractice McCorckel, was an important point.

Those two would be charged with capping in the head of the enemy column to hold the Reds up long enough to enjoy the full benefits of Black Eagle firepower. Four others in the Black Eagle Detachment —Falconi, Swift Elk, Top, and Gunnar—would provide the necessary fusillades to blow away the bulk of the enemy formation.

Archie Dobbs and Blue Richards had the same job that Buffalo Soldier and Malpractice had, except they would do it at the other end. They would stop up the front area to also keep the VC pressed within the main body's field of fire, and prevent any attempts at retreat.

Black Eagles didn't like the VC to ignore their invitations to an ambush.

In addition to that duty, Archie and Blue had to alert the others to any targets that might appear. If it looked good, the ambush would go down. If the force was too strong or made up of medical troops transporting wounded, or noncombatants such as women and children, Archie would call off the action until a better opportunity presented itself.

The fighting itself was designed to be short and deadly. The Black Eagles would empty at least two thirty-round magazines each into the enemy, then immediately break contact and pull back into the jungle. The idea behind the endeavor was to instill as much fear as physical casualty. This psychological effort could cause a great deal of reluctance on the part of heretofore casual supply convoys to travel happily and carefreely down that trail, knowing that potential killers lurked along each solitary meter of its distance.

Now Falconi thought it time for a commo check. He picked up his Prick-Six radio and spoke into it. "Nosey, this is Falcon. Over."

Archie quickly responded over his own communications gear. He involuntarily winced at the awful call sign that Top had assigned him. "Falcon, this is Nosey. Over."

"This is a commo check. How do you read me? Over."

"Five-by-five," Archie replied. "How you me? Over."

"Same," Falconi said. "Out."

Then the air over the detachment radios resumed hissing emptily through the receivers. Archie set his Prick-Six down and glanced up the trail. He turned and checked on Blue. The Alabamian, fifteen meters away, waved at him and winked.

Archie grinned and turned his attention back up the trail. The passing minutes seemed to slow down to crawling hours. Now and then the Black Eagle scout put his ear to the ground to see if he could detect any vibrations that would herald arriving travelers.

The afternoon eased by, the steamy heat markedly increasing in the thick vegetation Falconi and his men used for cover. Insects found them after a very short time and began buzzing around their ears and noses. They eased the plastic bottles of insect repellent from their pockets and applied it generously to their exposed skin.

Malpractice wiped some across his face. He knew the others would be doing the same, and he also had the added satisfaction of knowing they had brought the stuff because of his insistence. But he also realized that none of them would acknowledge his good actions. But somewhere, sometime, they would buy him a cold beer in some bar as a way of showing their gratitude for all that free medical advice and treatment he provided them. Malpractice decided that cold brews were better than verbal thank yous any day.

Back up at the front, Archie continued his ceaseless vigil. At exactly two hours and twenty-one minutes after the ambush had been organized, the scout sensed the approach of the enemy.

"Falcon," he said softly into the mouthpiece of the Prick-Six. "This is Nosey. Wait." He held his breath as the first man in a column of troops passed by. When the last man was in sight, Archie spoke again. "Two-zero victor Charlies," he reported. "I say again, two-zero victor Charlies. Good target. Hit 'em! Out."

Blue also had counted them. Two-zero victor Charlies meant twenty VC—a rifle section of enemy guerrillas. When the last Red walked past, Archie fell in at a discreet distance behind and followed. Blue waited for Archie to catch up with him. Then the two silently moved along in the rear of the enemy.

When the time was right they hurried forward to close up with the Charlies. Archie waited until the last man had turned into the bend in the trail. He squeezed the trigger on his M16, and Blue did the same. That trailing unfortunate caught the fired rounds in the shoulders and the back of his head. His body pitched forward lifeless in one blasting instant.

The battle was on!

Swift Elk and Falconi had already taken sight pictures on their targets. The first bullets bowled the VCs across the trail and into the brush on the other side. A couple behind them bolted forward in fear.

But they didn't go far.

Malpractice and the Buffalo Soldier cut them down before they could escape the zone of fire. Farther down the ambush, Top and Gunnar hosed the area in front of them with rapid semiautomatic sweeps of their M16s. Other rounds, coming in from Archie and Blue, joined theirs in a thundering swarm of steel-jacketed slugs.

In ten second it was all over.

The VC dead were sprawled grotesquely where they'd fallen. Pools of blood soaked into the soft jungle earth, while scarlet splatters covered the leaves of bushes and low-hanging tree branches.

Archie and Blue appeared on the trail. The scout looked at the carnage. "Jeez! That's some of the bloodiest work we've done in a while."

"I ain't never seen no ambush like it," Blue agreed.

Suddenly another volley of shots burst out.

"Gunnar!" Sergeant Major Top Gordon shouted. "Cease fire, goddamnit!"

Gunnar looked up from spraying the piles of enemy dead with his rifle. "Right, Top," he calmly said as he quit shooting.

Archie leaned close to Blue's ear and spoke softly. "Ol' Gunnar has a lot o' hate in him since Tiny bought the farm on the last mission, man."

"You're telling me!" Blue whispered back. "Them Scandahoovians brood a lot, and something has got to give in that situation or that boy is gonna bust wide open!"

Staff Sergeant Paulo Garcia, the detachment's intelligence specialist, did not waste any more time. He moved among the dead, rolling them over to check for insignia or other indications of rank and unit. He fished through the bloody, torn clothing on the cadavers and retrieved what documents he could. After a careful inspection, he threw them all away. "Nothing special. Just a bunch of fairly new recruits on their way to the war," he announced to Falconi.

"Are you pretty sure of that?" Falconi asked.

"Yeah," Paulo said. "Their uniforms—what's left of 'em, that is—are pretty new. Their web gear is used but clean and free of mildew. I'd say it was safe to assume those boys were replacements of some kind or another."

Swift Elk, also well-trained in military intelligence, agreed with the marine staff noncommissioned officer. "Right. They sure as hell haven't been out in the jungle long. And they didn't conduct themselves like veterans, either."

Falconi pulled a pack of cigarettes from his pocket. "At least they won't be shooting at any Americans at a later date." He looked at the smokes. "You know, I got to—"

"We know," Swift Elk interrupted. "You got to give those things up."

Falconi stuck one in his mouth and lit it. He winked at his second in command. "Fuck you, lieutenant."

"Fuck *you,* sir!" Swift Elk said, winking back.

"I hate to break up this here *tête-à-tête,*" Top said. "But if my memory serves me, we are out here on a mission, ain't we?"

"Tit-a-tit?" Archie asked. "What's that?"

"It ain't *tit-a-tit,* you dumb fucker," the sergeant major growled. "It's *tête-à-tête.* That's French for jawing together."

Archie laughed. "La-dee-da!"

"The Top's right," Falconi said. "Let's go search out more targets of opportunity that this theater of war has to offer us."

"What's next, sir?" Swift Elk asked.

Falconi shrugged. "That all depends on what Archie

95

finds for us."

"I can take a hint, sir," Archie said. He adopted a movie-hero type of voice. "Follow me, men!" he called out in a baritone. "I lead you to adventure, great fortune, and beautiful women!"

"Archie," the Buffalo Soldier said. "You jive-ass motherfucker! Just step out, huh? Never mind all the rest o' that shit."

"In that case," Archie said seriously, "follow me to hell itself. Because that's where I'm going to take you."

CHAPTER 8

Archie Dobbs, although traveling rapidly, moved with the stealth and grace of a stalking panther. Each step he took was a deliberate, conscious action as he continued to lead the detachment in a steady penetration deeper into the dangers of enemy territory.

The usual military topographical maps were virtually useless for finding man-made objects such as roads, buildings, and other forms of installations in the AO—Area of Operations. The Viet Cong and their big brothers in the North Vietnamese Army had moved into the territory in a big way. Using only hand tools and human labor, they had hacked supply routes and encampments in the deepest, least accessible parts of the jungle.

Archie, as the scout, could only utilize his map for natural features. Unless a hill had been leveled or a stream dammed, they still were located as displayed on the colored army charts, made out in a scale of 1:65,000.

Falconi fully realized this. After the ambush that had annihilated the VC infantry section, he'd given Archie specific instructions. "We don't know for sure what's out here," Falconi told him. "So we've got to guess at this point that there're roads, trails, rest camps, and other things the Charlies need to run supplies to the south."

Archie had been a bit discouraged. "Jesus, sir! The goddamned jungle is a big place. This is really searching for the needle in the haystack, ain't it?"

"Yeah," Falconi answered bluntly. "But you're just the guy to find that proverbial needle, aren't you?"

Archie grinned with pride. "Damn straight, sir!"

"Okay. So here's what we do," Falconi said, spreading his map out. "We'll make some educated guesses as to where the Charlies might decide to put in one of their versions of a freeway."

"I get you, sir," Archie said. "In other words, we should do like Swift Elk says and 'walk in their moccasins.' So we just look where we would build that kind of stuff if we were the bad guys, right?"

"Right."

Archie pointed to a spot on the map. "See that valley there? The contour lines around it are pretty close together, but the land between them is flat and friendly. But it's colored green, so that means plenty of vegetation. If I was a VC commander and I wanted to move some loads to my pals farther south, I'd use that as an easy place to put in a wide trail or even a damn good road. Not only could I move stuff pretty fast through there, I'd have plenty of cover from aerial observation on account o' that thick tree canopy."

"I agree," Falconi said. "Why don't you just take us up there and we'll take a look around."

Archie smiled. "I'll do that very thing sir. C'mon. Get the boys and follow me!"

Now, after moving the rest of that day, they were a few kilometers closer to the place they sought. The men followed Archie in single file. Each had an area of fire to cover. These defensive responsibilities alternated from left to right down the line. As the detachment moved along, each Black Eagle scanned the side of the trail he had been assigned to protect.

The roughest job was in the rear.

There, the last trooper had constantly to turn and cover the back of the formation. The men took turns at this, relieving each other every half hour as the slow, steady journey through enemy country continued.

A few hours later, Archie checked his watch and glanced up at the sky. In the tropics, the sunsets are fast and furious. The sun starts diving toward the far horizon and seems to gather up speed, while darkness descends like a falling black curtain.

Archie turned to his Prick-Six Radio. "Falcon. This is Nosey. Over."

"This is Falcon. Over," came back the reply.

"It'll be dark pretty quick," Archie said into the mouthpiece. "I'm at a good spot to bivouac. Let's bring the boys up and park here for the night. What do you say? Over."

"Roger that," Falconi said. "Stand fast. We're

coming up. Out."

Within ten minutes the entire detachment had caught up with their intrepid point man. Sergeant Major Top Gordon wasted no time in placing them out on a perimeter and ordering them to settle in for the night. The precise instructions were obeyed without comment. Suitable defensive positions for a possible night attack were prepared. Then creature comforts were looked after.

Jungle hammocks that could be rolled up tight enough to fit into the side pockets of a man's tiger fatigue trousers were produced and set up. These were enclosed with nylon covers and mosquito net sides. It would have been a tactical error to attach these to tree trunks in the regular fashion. Instead, the men erected them in the manner of small tents. After blowing up their air mattresses and arranging these and poncho liners for sleeping bags inside the hammocks' netting, they were ready for the coming night. This set-up gave them ground-level, insect-free sleeping arrangements. Once the guard roster was assigned, the men settled in to eat, nap, or pull their assigned sentry duties.

Top Gordon and Gunnar the Gunner were close together on one side of the perimeter. Top lit a cigar, enjoying the heavy taste of his smoke. He offered one to Gunnar.

"No thanks, Top," Gunnar said. "I don't even use cigarettes."

"The healthy blond Scandinavian, huh?" Top remarked with a grin.

"That's me," Gunnar said. He glanced around in the steamy heat at the green density of the jungle. "Sometimes I really feel I'm out of my element here in this part of the world. It ain't nothing like my ancestral home in Norway or my real one in Minnesota."

"Them Viking ancestors of yours ranged pretty far in their raiding," Top said. "But I reckon they never got to this part of the world."

"Nope," Gunnar said. "Even with good buddies like these around, I feel sort of lost."

Top knew what was bugging the young soldier. He decided brutal frankness would be much kinder than gentle politeness. "Especially since Tiny Burke got killed, huh?"

Gunnar grimaced. "Yeah," he said softly. "That was a real *kniv inn ryggen.*"

"What?" Top asked.

"Excuse me," Gunnar said. "That means 'knife in the back' in Norwegian. Sometimes I slip into the language without thinking. We speak it at home, thanks to my *foreldre*—er—my parents."

Top realized this was a time to get him talking. He asked a question he already knew the answer to, but with the idea of opening up the brooding Scandinavian. "Where'd you meet ol' Tiny, anyhow?"

"He was a loader and mechanic's helper in my old chopper squadron," Gunnar said. "That's where I was the gunner on my cousin's gunship. You remember Warrant Officer Erick Stensland, don't you?"

"I sure do," Top said. "He pulled our asses out of it a couple of times."

"Tiny tended to our chopper," Gunnar went on. "He was kinda dumb, y'know? But what he lacked in brains he made up in brawn and balls. When I volunteered for a transfer to the Black Eagles, he wanted to come along. At first I told him he couldn't, but he got real hurt. Then I realized he would be a good ammo bearer for me when Colonel Falconi told me I'd be carrying an M60."

"You were right about that," Top agreed.

"If I'd made him stay with the chopper outfit, he'd still be alive," Gunnar said.

"You didn't make him stay there," Top said. "And, on the other hand, you didn't make him come with you. He wanted to, that's all."

"I guess I never considered it in that way," Gunnar said.

"Tiny really thought a lot of you," Top said. "I think the guy would've been miserable if you'd left him back at your old outfit."

Gunnar nodded. "Yeah. Me and Tiny were friends. He had trouble figuring things out sometimes. He always asked my advice. I really brought him into the shit though, didn't I?"

"Hell, Gunnar! Tiny might have gotten killed during a raid on your airfield or something," Top said. "A man don't have to be with the Black Eagles to die in Vietnam."

Gunnar smiled sardonically. "That's for damn sure."

Top now thought the conversation had gone far enough. Gunnar had opened up just the right amount. It would take a couple of more times, but the young soldier would soon feel better. "I'm going to catch a catnap before midnight," Top said. "Then I'll go out and make a check of the whole perimeter."

"Yeah. And I got guard in a coupla more hours," Gunnar said. He went to his hammock and crawled under the netting. He turned back and looked at the detachment's senior noncommissioned officer. "You got a way of putting things right. It was nice talking with you, sergeant major."

"It was nice talking to you, Gunnar," Top said, settling down onto his own bedding.

The Black Eagles went into the nighttime routine. Sentries were changed every two hours in silent guard mounts that took place in near total darkness. The men slept on their time off, slumping into shallow naps from which they would recover to full wakefulness at the slightest sound. Once they realized nothing was wrong, they would once again resume their light sleeping syndrome.

Top had a built-in biological sergeant's clock somewhere deep in his psyche. It never failed him. A few moments before dawn, he always awoke. His first action would be to run a perimeter check on the men on duty, then start waking the others up. Noise discipline was strictly observed during this informal, inelegant reveille. Although now and then some wise guy would emit a loud C-ration fart that caused muffled chuckling among the others.

Within a short half-hour the entire detachment was on its feet, fully fed, loaded up, and moving out to meet the day's challenges.

Archie resumed his task of leading the men toward that valley to see what might be there. The detachment followed, covering their fields of fire in case of ambush, always ready for the unexpected with an eagerness born of their naturally aggressive and unfriendly attitude toward strangers.

A fast-running stream of refreshing cold water was discovered at midmorning. It was not on the map, and it was easy to see why. It was covered with overlying branches and deep jungle grass. The cartographer who had made the chart used by Archie would have had to have been on the ground to spot it, rather than drawing from an aerial photograph.

The men emptied their canteens of the tepid, stale water they had been carrying and refilled them with the fresh cool liquid of the tiny creek. They soaked their boonie hats in it, poured it over their uniforms, and drank until their bellies sloshed. This was done at Malpractice's insistence. He wanted them to replace the water they'd lost through heavy perspiring for the previous couple of days. He capped it all off by issuing salt tablets and watching to make sure each man took at least two.

After the refreshing pause, Archie went back to work. He took the unit along the base of a steep, long hill and brought them up on the opposite side of the valley. When they were near the crest, they halted. Falconi came forward. He motioned to Top and Swift Elk. "Hold the guys here while Archie and I move to the top and take a look down there."

"You got it, sir," Top said. He turned around and looked at the men. "Who told you jokers to take a break? Get to your defensive positions *now!*"

The men scrambled around to arrange themselves to meet any attacks that might hit them. Even then Top wasn't satisfied. He personally inspected each place, changing things around to suit his own particular tastes in defense.

"Paulo! Clear that brush in front of you. You're the automatic rifle here. You'll need plenty of room to swing that M16 in an attack!"

"Get lower, Buffalo Soldier!"

"Malpractice! Move to the other side of that bush!"

"C'mon, Gunnar! You can do better than that!"

"Hey, Blue! Get outta that tree! If you get shot you're gonna fall on top of Buffalo Soldier."

Buffalo Soldier Culpepper glanced up and grinned. "Yeah! You don't want me to get hurt do you, Blue?"

"If they shoot my ass outta here, I won't give a shit if I land on your butt or not," Blue said, easing down the tree trunk to the ground.

"That's what you think," Top growled. "Your last dying impression will be of me kicking your tail!"

Lieutenant Ray Swift Elk, comfortable in the middle of the defensive circle, smiled. "I'm sure as hell glad I got a commission," he said to himself as he watched the sergeant major enforce his standards of defense on the men.

Meanwhile, Falconi and Archie edged onward to the top of the hill. Falconi started to pull his binoculars from the case on his pistol belt, but he stopped. "For the love of God!"

"Shit, sir!" Archie exclaimed.

Down below them, stretching like a ribbon slashed into the jungle greenery, was a wide road. Hardpacked and well constructed, it would have done credit to any rural county back in the U.S.A.

"There's a bridge, Archie," Falconi said. "See it?"

Archie retrieved his own binoculars. "Yes, sir! It's easy to see the thing is capable of supporting trucks. Them Reds is moving more stuff through here than G2 knew about."

"I think we ought to blow up that bridge," Falconi said softly.

Archie grinned. "Buffalo Soldier and Blue will be

105

glad to hear that."

"Let me qualify that last statement," Falconi said. "We ought to blow up that bridge when there is a truck convoy crossing it."

"Now *that* would be interesting!" Archie said.

"Let's get back to the detachment," Falconi said.

The two eased back from their observation point and retraced their steps through the jungle. Ray Swift Elk, waiting for them, came forward. "You guys look like the cat that swallowed the canary."

"We sure as hell have," Falconi said. He motioned to Archie. "Fetch Buffalo Soldier and Blue up here. And get Gunnar, too. We've got to arrange for a supply drop of C4 explosive."

Swift Elk watched Archie disappear into the foliage to tend to the chore. He looked back at Falconi. "It seems there's the beginning of a little operation going on here."

"Yeah," Falconi agreed. "The next couple of days are going to be real exciting around here." He pulled out a cigarette and lit it. "No shit, guys, I've got to give these things up."

CHAPTER 9

Falconi could hear the aircraft droning toward them in the distance. Paulo Garcia, in the radio broadcast prepared by Gunnar Olson, had already given the pilot the exact grid coordinates of the drop zone, and the azimuth on which the aviator should fly. Now all the detachment commander could hope was for that information to be accurately and quickly utilized by the navigator.

The area they had chosen for the delivery had been picked rather dangerously. Without time for a thorough physical reconnaissance, Falconi had relied entirely on his map. Using his scale and knowledge of topographical symbols, he selected a place that seemed to be flat and open enough to accommodate the badly needed supply drop. At the same time, it also had to be far enough from the target bridge that any discovery of the operation would not result in a saturation of enemy troops into the area.

To add to the suspense, the actual coordinates of the drop zone had also been worked out on paper ahead of time.

All in all, it was a hell of a chance to take, but Falconi didn't have time to send a reconnaissance patrol to leisurely check the place out. When the detachment finally arrived on the site, they were happy to find the terrain perfect for an aerial delivery.

Whether it was really safe from enemy observation and action remained to be seen.

Gunnar, as supply sergeant, had arranged for the proper packaging of the requested goods. He had worked with Paulo Garcia in setting up the coded message that was sent back in Morse Code. Broken down into five-letter word groups, the short broadcast had given the G4 office at SOG all the information they needed regarding this supply requisition to be delivered into enemy territory.

Now, with the airplane closing in on them, Buffalo Soldier suddenly had a slightly disturbing thought. He walked over to Gunnar and sat down. "If something goes wrong, them caps in the bundle might explode. Did you tell 'em to keep the fuses and caps separate from the C4?"

"Hell, yes!" Gunnar said. "This is a drag-chute drop. That stuff won't be floating down from the sky under big parachute canopies. I know better than to have the detonators and explosives all mixed up together."

"I'm just checking," Buffalo Soldier said. "In my line o' work, you can't be too careful."

"I admire your professionalism," Gunnar said. "But don't worry. Everything is set up perfect."

Top gestured at them and hissed. "Shut up! The Falcon has got to be able to hear his radio."

Falconi leaned close to the receiver, listening for the voice of the pilot, who was drawing closer. In a case like this, there would be but one time to pass over the drop zone and deliver the goods. There was too much opportunity for a flying aircraft to attract the attention of nearby enemy units. The consequences of such an occurrence would mean a deadly compromise of the detachment if the supply drop took too much time in the necessity of having the approach repeated.

The radio abruptly crackled to life, the pilot asking the challenge. "Eagle. This is aircraft. Token. Token. Token. Over."

Falconi responded quickly and correctly. "Aircraft. This is Eagle. Card. Card. Card. Over."

"Affirmative, Eagle. The run-in is underway. We'll be flying in at one-zero-zero knots at an altitude of six-five-zero above ground level. It's going to be tight. Give the word when it's right to execute. Over."

"Roger," Falconi said into the mouthpiece. He waited as the aircraft, a C-123, could be heard dropping lower and lower through the dense tropical air. Suddenly it burst into view over the treeline above them. The Black Eagle commander timed it perfectly. "Execute! Execute! Execute!"

A pair of door bundles fell from the aircraft. Immediately, two drag chutes deployed, giving the cargo a semiguided trip to the ground. The drop zone detail, Malpractice, Blue, and Archie rushed out to the open area to pick up the packages of explosive and detonation paraphernalia. Within a short minute they had returned to the treeline.

Unfortunately, it was at that exact moment that a VC patrol stumbled into the area.

The Buffalo Soldier was the first to sight them. From their antics, he knew they had seen everything. He whipped his M16 to his shoulder and sprayed their tight formation. Two of the Charlies buckled under the volley, but their buddies broke back to the safety of the jungle.

Ray Swift Elk, realizing any escapees would give away information on the Black Eagles, yelled out, "Top! Gunnar! Go to the north! We've got to catch up and cut 'em off! Try to get around the sons-of-bitches!" He gestured wildly to Calvin Culpepper. "C'mon, Buffalo Soldier! We'll take the southern route."

Paulo Garcia, who had been spared from working with the retrieval party because of his hurt hand, left the other side of the drop zone. He ran across the open field as fast as he could go to catch up with the pursuers.

As Paulo rushed to join their efforts, the four chasers crashed through the jungle. It was a horribly dangerous situation. If they slowed down to probe forward in case of a potential ambush, they might very well lose their quarry in the event the Viet Cong decided to run for freedom. On the other hand, the amount of noise they were making set them up as irresistible targets if the Charlies decided to stop and take cover.

110

The circumstances called for only one conclusion. A big chance had to be taken. It could well be worth a life or two if the Red guerrillas were stopped from getting back to their unit and reporting the incident of an enemy supply drop.

Both Swift Elk and Top reached that deduction independently of each other even before the wild dash to encircle the enemy patrol and annihilate it.

Top and Gunnar tried to stay in sight of each other, but it was impossible in the dense jungle. Top, on the inside position closest to the Charlies, kept glancing back and forth in wild hopes of seeing the enemy and/or Gunnar. His first fruitful glance was that of a black-pajama-clad jungle fighter wearing a conical cap. Top snapped off a hasty shot.

The Charlie, wild-eyed with fright and anger, stopped and swung to face the American. The AK47 sounded a blasting chunka-chunka of firing. Top could feel the rounds splitting the air around his head. He took a quick, but careful aim and squeezed the trigger three times.

The first bullet did nothing but zing off into the foliage. The second hit the mark, however, causing the VC involuntarily to throw up his hands and toss the assault rifle in the air at the same moment that the third bullet split open his face.

Top didn't wait to watch the man fall. He turned and renewed his wild running.

Buffalo Soldier ran like a wild man. His eyes were open wide in the excitement of the pursuit as his African warrior heritage guided him in the automatic actions of pure instinct. He turned inward toward

111

where he guessed the Reds might have gotten themselves in their dash for freedom.

Buffalo Soldier burst through a stand of bamboo and collided with a VC going at a full run. Both crashed to the ground as their weapons somersaulted off through the air to land in the bushes several meters away.

The Charlie was on his feet first. He hissed and kicked out at Buffalo Soldier, causing the American to roll back out of the way. The enemy guerrilla spun on his heel and took off again. Buffalo Soldier scrambled up and chased after the man. The chase went on for another twenty meters of crashing through thorns, limbs, and brush. Then the VC whipped around and stopped, a machete he'd carried in a scabbard on his back now drawn and ready.

Buffalo Soldier couldn't slow down. He decided to pick up a bit of speed to increase his momentum. When the Charlie swung the razor-sharp weapon, the Black Eagle dove inside the move, driving the heel of his hand straight into the enemy's chin. At the same time, he reached out and grabbed the man's wrist, twisting sharply. Buffalo Soldier followed this with a beautifully executed spin, putting his back to his adversary while he deftly grabbed the machete and took it for his own. He continued the whirling motion until he once again faced the enemy soldier.

The blade whistled through the air, the arc ending with a horrible crack as it split the Red's skull.

Less than twenty meters away, so close and yet unable to see the drama that had occurred, Swift Elk also pulled a one-man attack. He had actually spotted his prey, but he was unable to make some quick maneuvers to get ahead of the guy.

Swift Elk stopped behind a tree and fought his breath to bring it under control. His eyes nearly watered from the effort, but the Black Eagle could hear the VC drawing closer, kicking up a fuss in his frantic bid for escape. When the time was right, Swift Elk stepped out from his cover and almost froze.

Instead of one Charlie, there were three!

The AK47 fire sounded like the blasting roar of a jet engine to the Sioux Indian's ears. All he could do was shoot back. With his selector on semiautomatic, his trigger finger had to pull down with the rapidity of a speed typist at work.

Leaves, bits of branches, spiraling hunks of tree bark, and dust raised by the concussion filled the air.

The nearest VC's chest suddenly exploded in a crimson mass, causing the man to stagger backward to fall. Swift Elk's boonie hat made a half turn on his head and a quarter of the brim flew away.

The second Charlie abruptly dropped to the ground, but the third hung in there. He fired with the same grim determination that Swift Elk demonstrated—until his left ear was blown from his head. He instinctively turned with the impact of the round, and Swift Elk's continual fire paid off with a hit to the throat.

The firefight, which had taken four seconds, ended as quickly as it had begun.

Gunnar Olson was the farthest man out. He had heard plenty of shooting, but had yet to see even a fleeting target to shoot at. The jungle had suddenly grown eerily quieter, and he felt an uncomfortable chill that caused him to shudder involuntarily.

"Yaaaaaah!"

The scream of rage split the air as the Red burst into view, making a one-man bayonet charge straight at Gunnar. "What's this, then?" he asked himself.

"Yaaaaaah!"

Gunnar slowly raised his M16 to his shoulder and took a good sight picture at the man running toward him.

"Yaaaaaah!" The Charlie continued his wild battle cry of rage and defiance.

The Black Eagle squeezed the trigger, feeling the rifle push back into his shoulder.

"Aaaaaa—uuuuh!" The charge ended in an undignified tumble to the muddy soil, blood splattering the nearby plants.

Gunnar started to relax at the sight of the dead man. But he heard sounds behind him. He turned abruptly and dropped down to his knee.

"Easy," Paulo Garcia said. "It's me."

Gunnar stood up. "The crazy bastard ran straight at me with his frigging bayonet. You should've seen him!"

"I did," Paulo said. He walked over and examined the cadaver. "He's what you'd call hardcore, right?"

"About like them Red Bears we went up against in the last operation," Gunnar said.

Top Gordon now joined them. He gave the corpse a quick glance. "That's the last one. Let's get back to the Falcon and the others."

When the chasers rejoined their comrades, Swift Elk delivered a concise, accurate report to the detachment commander. "We got 'em all, sir."

"Good," Falconi said. "But we're still not home free yet. The enemy knows we're in the area. They must've found those jokers we ambushed yesterday. And they probably heard all the shooting here. We can't take time to bury the enemy stiffs, so their comrades will surely find what's left of that patrol. So let's move fast before dark. I want to set up a base camp, then blow that bridge first chance in the morning."

Archie Dobbs, always aware of his environment, spoke up. "We'd best rush it, sir. It'll be dark pretty quick."

Top Gordon knew his job as senior noncommissioned officer. He looked at the waiting men. "Well! Goddamnit, don't just stand there! Move out!"

Hours later, when the Black Eagles had settled into their night routine, a small drama unfolded.

Saigon was curtained deeply in the dark of night, when the telephone in Chuck Fagin's apartment rang. The jangling noise penetrated the sleep and whiskey fog that clouded his brain.

His grasp of the receiver was instinctive, but he was wide awake by the time he spoke the code words:

"Charleston."

The voice on the other end was just as terse: "Bloomer. One-five minutes. I say again, Bloomer. One-five minutes."

Then the line went dead.

115

Fagin groaned and forced himself from bed. The air conditioner in the window hummed as he struggled into the rumpled clothing he had cast off only two hours previously. He dressed and hurriedly tied his shoes. Then the CIA case officer slipped the Colt .380 automatic pistol into the holster on his belt. After flopping his shirttail over the weapon, he grabbed his hat, heading for the door.

The lobby of the apartment building was protected by a pair of armed ARVN military policemen who stood outside the iron grille that covered the entrance. Fagin called to them:

"Xin loi ong!"

They turned, recognizing him immediately. *"Chao ong,* Ong Fagin," the senior called out. He walked over and unlocked the gate.

"Howdy," Fagin said, stepping out onto the sidewalk. He looked up at the bleak, dark sky in which the stars looked pale and washed out. In a few weeks the monsoon season would arrive, and that celestial picture would be one of flashing lightning and thundering black clouds.

"You go out, Ong Fagin?"

"Yeah," Fagin answered. "I have some business to attend to."

"So late in the *ban dem?"* the MP said. "Important man always busy, eh?"

"That's right," Fagin said. He glanced down the street in time to see the military sedan turn the corner and race toward them. "This is my ride, fellahs. *Chao ong!"*

They waved good-bye as Fagin waited for the car to

pull up to the curb. He quickly got into the back seat. The driver wasted no time in hitting the accelerator and racing off down the avenue.

The ride was uneventful and silent. They turned into the gate at Peterson Field. Fagin was let out at a special side door of the main building. After showing his ID to the guards there, he was admitted, and he entered to walk down a long hall to an elevator. After another identity inspection, he got inside the conveyance and was whisked up to the third floor.

Brigadier General John Taggart had been waiting impatiently in his office. When Fagin came in, the general wasted no time with formalities. He pointed to another officer in the room. "I think you know Johnson, right?"

Fagin smiled a greeting. "Hello, Johnny! Long time no see."

"You're looking good, Chuck," Lieutenant Colonel Johnson said. "I hear you're the case officer for Falconi's Black Eagles."

"That's right," Fagin answered. "What are you up to?"

"I've just been assigned here as G2," Johnson answered. "I just got here, but it seems that things happen fast in this part of the world."

Taggart was anxious to get down to business. "You two old pals can shoot the shit later," he snapped. "Johnson is here to give a report."

Fagin nodded. "I assume it concerns the Black Eagles, right?"

"Exactly," Johnson answered. "Highly reliable sources have informed us that an extremely heavy

117

concentration of North Vietnamese troops are moving into the Black Eagles' area of operation."

"It's all confirmed," Taggart said. He motioned to Johnson. "Use the map on the wall and brief him."

Johnson spent the next half hour tracing the movements of various NVA units. Their routes of travel showed that every one was converging into the territory where the Black Eagles were operating.

"Jesus Christ!" Fagin explained. "The place is saturated with the bastards."

"That's why we're radioing Falconi and ordering an immediate cessation of the mission," Taggart said. "We've got to get his ass out of there."

Fagin walked over to the general's desk and helped himself to a cigar from the humidor there. "Suppose Falconi don't want to be exfiltrated?" he asked, biting off the end.

"Well, Fagin, he'd damned well better want to be!" Taggart said. "Because we sure as hell aren't sending any more supply drops into there. We can't take those kinds of chances with expensive airplanes."

"He'll be up to his ass in NVA, Fagin," Johnson added. "We've really got to get him and his men clear of the area ASAP. If we don't, you can start packing their personal effects for shipment home now."

"In fact," Taggart added, "he'd damned well better be laying low right now. If the Black Eagles are out kicking up some shit, it might just be too late to save their asses."

"I haven't heard any reports from Falconi," Fagin said calmly. "But he's requested a demolition supply drop. I'll bet my last ten bucks that he is raising some kind of hell out in the AO."

Taggart shrugged. "Then our radio broadcast might not be picked up by his commo man." He took one of his own cigars. "It's been my experience that dead radio operators rarely answer when they're raised on the net."

CHAPTER 10

Dawn was only a hint of pink high up in the thick foliage of the tallest trees as Malpractice McCorckel crawled under the thick brush along the side of the river. He situated himself as best he could for observation, then withdrew the binoculars from the case on the back of his pistol belt.

Malpractice made sure the focus was good and sharp, then peered through the double lenses. He swept the local area with a slow, steady gaze. He studied the riverbank on both sides of the wide, muddy tributary, but the medical sergeant gave special attention to the bridge a hundred meters downstream. After twenty minutes of this careful study, he replaced the binoculars, and withdrew back into the jungle.

Falconi, situated within the perimeter of the unit's defensive position, was waiting for him. "So, how does it look, Malpractice?"

"Damned good, sir. There ain't even any guards on the bridge."

"I didn't think there would be," Falconi said. "The Viet Cong are undoubtedly now aware that someone is prowling in the middle of their territory, but they don't rate us as much of a threat yet. At least not enough to make them worry about that goddamned bridge."

"Buffalo Soldier and Blue will make 'em change their minds on that point," Malpractice said.

"Unfortunately, that's a situation we've got to face up to. Once that bridge is blown," Falconi said ominously, "then things are bound to get tougher around here. Even if the bastards don't come gunning for us, they'll triple their security procedures. That'll mean any sneak-and-peek operation will be a hell of a lot more difficult."

"We've been through all that before, sir," Malpractice reminded the commander.

"Yeah. Anyway, we're wasting time. Get on back with the others and send our demo team up here," Falconi said.

"Yes, sir," Malpractice said.

He went back deeper into the jungle where the rest of the detachment waited. He found Buffalo Soldier Culpepper and Blue Richards waiting. They had a flotation device made of ponchos stretched over a frame of tree branches sitting between them. They had constructed the affair the previous evening in the day's last dull gleams of sunlight.

"It looks good," Malpractice told them. "The old

122

man wants to see you."

The two got to their feet and moved forward, carrying the small raft with them. They found Falconi twenty meters ahead. "Malpractice says we can do it, sir," Buffalo Soldier said. "Things are looking good, huh?"

"Right," Falconi confirmed. "The bridge is to your right. There's no sentries on it, but be careful."

"Aye, aye, sir," Blue said. He nudged his partner. "C'mon, Buffalo Soljer. We got a bridge to tear up."

The two went down to the water's edge. After stripping off their uniforms, they lowered the floating device into the water and went in after it. Swimming slowly and cautiously, they let the current edge them up to the bridge.

"Shit, man!" Buffalo Soldier said. "Will you look at that baby?"

"Dawgies!" Blue exclaimed. "When you get close to this thing, you can see how good it's really made."

"I'll tell you, man," Buffalo Soldier said. "There was a first class engineer involved in building this beauty."

"Yeah?" Blue remarked. "Well, there's some real primo demo guys involved in bringing her down."

"Right on!"

"Let's hit four of these lower braces," Blue said. "That'll bring the whole kitten-kaboodle down into the river.

Without any further talk, the pair set to work. Blue reached over and grabbed a long uncut length of demo wire and a blasting cap. He set the cap over the line and crimped it tight to keep it from slipping out. After checking the lay of the wire, he slipped it into a one-pound block of C4 explosive.

123

"Let's get fancy and use diamond packs. We can aim 'em toward the other side," Blue suggested. "It'll take out both sets of supports that way."

"Blue, when you're right, you're right!" Buffalo Soldier said with a grin.

They worked steadily from that point on, without talking. Each was an individual, although they practiced teamwork in the destructive undertaking their commander had assigned them. They glanced up once when the rest of the detachment showed up on the bridge. Gunnar Olson and Paulo Garcia waved down to them, displaying grins. "Hey! Don't you two jokers blow this thing up with us on it, you hear?"

Gunnar added his own humor. "Yeah. The army'll deduct our pay for the time we spend up in the air."

"You two!" came the sergeant major's angry voice. "Knock it off!"

Gunnar and Paulo were roughly grabbed by Top Gordon and hustled back to ambush positions on the roadway that led off the bridge.

Buffalo Soldier and Blue grinned at each other over the sergeant major's impatience with their buddies, then went back to their task. Within a half hour the project was done. Now they swam back to the riverbank, Blue pulling the flotation gear while Calvin carefully unstrung the demo wire on each of the four charges.

Once they reached the bank, they dismantled the raft. Blue retrieved his poncho and rolled it up while Buffalo Soldier unraveled the remainder of the wire. He worked his way up the bank and onto the road. After moving a scant fifteen meters into the brush, he stopped.

Blue, now with the poncho rolled and attached to his patrol harness, joined him. He pulled the detonators out of his backpack. "Let's hook 'em up."

The two demolitions experts slipped the end of the wire into the connections on the detonators and screwed them down tight. Buffalo Soldier, knowing where Falconi was supposed to be located, waved in that direction. The detachment commander came out of the jungle and crossed the road to join them.

"We can bring that baby down anytime you say, sir," Buffalo Soldier said.

"Good," Falconi said. "We're going to wait for one of those truck convoys to come along. We might as well kill two birds with one stone, as the old cliche goes, and Gunnar says we might be able to pick up some useful loot out of the blasted trucks. Supply drops can be a real problem sometimes."

"You created a Frankenstein when you made that Minnesota boy the supply sergeant," Blue said. "All he thinks about is stores and goods."

"Scandinavians are as tight as Scots," Falconi said. He pointed up toward the bridge. "Can you see Malpratice up there?"

Blue and Buffalo Soldier both looked in the indicated direction. Malpractice, easily seen from that angle, waved at them.

"When he gives the signal to let her rip," Falconi said, "you two crank those detonator handles."

"And we'll fire four electrically," Blue said. He looked at Buffalo Soldier. "That's sailor talk, man."

"I thought y'all said things like 'pipe the admiral through the porthole' and 'swab the poopdeck with the bos'un,'" Buffalo Soldier said.

125

"Naw," Blue assured him. "We don't never say nothing like that."

"You two stop the jawing and pay attention to Malpractice," Falconi ordered.

"Aye, aye, sir!"

"Yes, sir!"

Falconi left them and rejoined Swift Elk in their position at the edge of the road. Up forward, well concealed and waiting, Malpractice settled in to sweat out the arrival of an enemy convoy.

The day's heat eased into high intensity as the hours dragged by. Once again, the weather played havoc with the detachment's physical comfort. The sun, so pretty and pink before, was now a blazing disk of white hell in the sky above. Its scorching warmth pounded down on the jungle, making the moisture in the soil float upward in an unseen vapor of wet heat.

Malpractice wiped at the stinging perspiration that seeped into his eyes. His uniform, sticky and wet hot, stuck to his skin. His underarms and crotch felt like they were covered with a red, burning rash. His throat was dry, and his lips felt like they were about to crack open from the high temperature.

Then he abruptly forgot the discomfort.

The distant whine of truck motors was easily heard in the distance. He made a hasty wave of his hand to catch the attention of Buffalo Soldier and Blue. When they signaled back to him, Malpractice gave his full attention to the happenings to his direct front.

The sound grew steadily, but maddeningly slowly, as the convoy approached. After a few minutes a Soviet-made GAZ-63 truck came into view. At first Malpractice was afraid it would stop and a detachment of troops would get out to inspect the bridge. But the vehicle continued forward at a 30 mph pace.

When it reached the bridge, Malpractice raised his hand.

Now he could see there were other trucks and all were cargo type. No troops occupied the backs of the vehicles. That was just what Gunnar Olson wanted.

There were only four of the vehicles. They continued forward until the first almost reached the end of the bridge and was ready to roll out onto the road.

Malpractice dropped his hand.

Back in their position, Buffalo Soldier and Blue quickly cranked a detonator each, then grabbed another to repeat the action. The results of their efforts were four big explosions that lifted the bridge and its cargo high into the air before dropping them down to the river below.

"Let's go!" Top Gordon bellowed.

The entire detachment, with weapons at the ready, rushed forward. When they reached the edge of the ruined bridge they stared down at the wreckage below. The four trucks, two of them burning upside down on the riverbank, were bunched below. The middle trucks could barely be seen beneath the surface of the muddy water of the river.

"Let's get down there and see if there is anything worth taking," Falconi ordered.

"Yes, sir," Top said. He pointed to Archie and Malpractice. "You two go up on the other side and make sure nobody joins our party." He beckoned to the others. "Ever'body else! C'mon, let's get some goodies."

There was a scramble as the men went to the tasks.

The inspection of the vehicles showed that they were

127

not badly damaged. They would certainly never be driven again, but structurally, they were only bent and twisted from the fall. The cargo, lashed down under canvas, seemed also to be in good shape. A half-dozen buck knives slashed through the restraining ropes on the exposed trucks, and the tarpaulins were pulled back.

"Mortar ammo!" someone called out.

A search of both loads ensued. After numerous crates were broken open, Top reported back to Falconi. "Sir. This here stuff is 82 millimeter shells for Russian mortars."

Falconi looked over at Swift Elk. "What do you make of that?"

Swift Elk shrugged. "I don't know, sir. That seems like pretty big stuff for the Viet Cong. They usually use smaller weaponry, even in support."

Paulo Garcia, as the intelligence sergeant, had not spent a moment with the freight. Instead, he had concentrated his efforts on searching the corpses of the enemy drivers. He had even stripped off his clothing and dived into the river to drag the dead men from the sunken trucks. After depositing the cadavers on the bank, he calmly dressed, then went about searching the bodies.

He found manifests and ID papers, and those findings disturbed him a great deal. He took the items over to Swift Elk and Falconi. "I don't like this shit."

"What's the matter?" Falconi asked.

"Look, sir. Manifests of the loads, right down to the last fucking crate," Paulo said. "All neatly entered on the proper forms. And another thing—them stiffs got ID papers."

"Holy shit!" Swift Elk exclaimed. "And to top it off, it was all done on typewriters."

"Yes, sir," Paulo said. "And you'll notice the manifests are all numbered."

"I'll bet those match the packing slips in the cases, too," Swift Elk said.

The detachment commander was irritated by his inability to understand what the two military intelligence experts were getting at. "What the hell is the matter with you two?" Falconi demanded.

"Sir, these guys and those trucks are not Viet Cong," Swift Elk explained. His own background in military intelligence was even more sophisticated than Paulo's. "Those identity cards and the manifest forms are from the North Vietnamese Army."

"The NVA?" Falconi exclaimed. "This is supposed to be strictly a VC operation out here."

"Look at their uniforms, sir," Paulo said. "It's a little difficult to tell from here because they're soaking wet, but that clothing is well-made green fatigue-type stuff."

Heavy gunfire suddenly sounded above them.

All looked up to see both Archie and Malpractice scrambling down the riverbank. "NVA!" Archie yelled. "We're being hit by NVA, for Chrissake!"

CHAPTER 11

Spurts of dirt from incoming AK47 rounds kicked up around their feet as Archie Dobbs and Malpractice McCorckel made a wild, running descent down from the roadbed amid the roaring chaos created by the blasting enemy weaponry.

"Cover 'em!" Top Gordon ordered as he cut loose with a fusillade at the green-clad North Vietnamese army troops appearing above the two fleeing Black Eagles. The other detachment members instantly obeyed. They began returning the fire even at the same instant that they dove behind what little cover was offered along the riverbank.

Several of the NVA, anxious for shots at the fugitives, paid for their impetuous pursuit by catching the full brunt of the preliminary volleys. Whipped by the swarm of Black Eagle bullets, they tumbled off the road and slid grotesquely down to the water's edge, their assault rifles clattering after them. A couple, badly hit, screamed in shock and pain until some of their more daring buddies rushed forward to pull them out of harm's way.

Falconi's men enjoyed a brief advantage at this preliminary part of the battle.

The attackers were not aware of what faced them from below. Their initial rush slowed to a few hesitant probes as the Red squad leaders gained more control over their young, eager soldiers. Once a semblance of order had been established, the senior NVA men made a quick visual reconnaissance of the Americans' position.

It took them only ten minutes to correctly surmise what the situation was for the defenders down at the river. These invaders were firmly locked in between the bluff and the riverbed.

Now, fully apprised of the battle's circumstances, the NVA commander wisely ordered his men to take advantage of the cover along the top of the riverbank. He screamed orders at his section and squad leaders to move their units into the best possible combat positions. Once the Reds were situated, they began a coordinated return fire that plowed into the Black Eagles.

Falconi was doing his own impromptu planning. He quickly realized that he and the others would be fatally pinned down in a matter of short moments. If this were to happen, there would be no chance for escape. The entire unit would be shot to pieces like clay pigeons at a trap shoot.

"Break to the right!" he yelled out. "Go for it!"

Paulo Garcia led the charge. The pain from his injured hand was only a dull sensation in his combat-fevered mind as he pumped out firebursts of a half-dozen rounds at a time. His efforts cost one NVA his life, and forced the man's squad mates instinctively to duck their heads.

"Go! Go!" Swift Elk yelled as he pounded away directly behind the marine.

All the detachment's firepower was directed upward and forward as they covered themselves with a curtain of 5.56 millimeter slugs. Archie Dobbs was the one exception. The scout was so anxious to get into his regular place at the head of the column that he damned the danger and ran like a crazed man toward the front. He weaved in and out among his buddies, sometimes bumping into one of them, until he finally passed Paulo.

Archie crashed ahead, trying to pick out the best possible route out of the area. But his efforts were suddenly stymied.

A section of NVA infantry that had pulled away from the main body had left the higher ground and made their way down from the roadbed in order to make an enveloping movement. They had done this in the hopes of springing a surprise attack on the riverbank itself. They were as shocked to see Archie as he was to see them.

But he reacted quicker.

He dumped the leading trio of Reds with a half-dozen hip shots as he backed away. Taking advantage of the enemy's momentary confusion, he turned and raced back to the detachment, which had just appeared.

"There's more of 'em up there," Archie yelled out to Falconi in the middle of the formation. "The path along the river is too narrow. They own the frigging thing."

"Goddamnit!" Falconi swore. He signaled to Swift Elk and Top Gordon. "Take 'em back. We're cut off from going farther in this direction."

The detachment retraced their steps, returning to the blasted trucks. Their initial disappointment was swept away at a sight they hadn't expected. The NVA who had sought to pin them up like a herd of cattle were now scrambling down to the river in a wild attempt to close in on the Americans. Awkward on the steep incline, their footing was precarious as they stumbled clumsily in their descent.

"Fish in a barrel!" Buffalo Soldier called out.

Nine M16s blasted away for thirty seconds, sweeping the ravine clean of enemy troops. The NVA dead and wounded rolled down to the water. Some remained on the bank, but others continued on into the river. Any helpless injured were sure of drowning. Their more fortunate buddies scrambled back to the top for the safety the jungle covering offered on the higher terrain.

Falconi and his men moved into positions around the trucks and kept up the fusillades for as long as they could.

Then the NVA heavy machine guns entered the battle. These were big Soviet DShK killing mechanisms that threw out ponderous 12.7 millimeter slugs.

Sparks and pings flew off the vehicles' metal bodies as the slugs slapped into the Black Eagle position.

Archie Dobbs and Blue Richards attempted to return fire, but all they accomplished was to attract the attention of the NVA gunners. The increased incoming rounds forced the pair to duck back behind cover.

"Them bastards is getting serious!" Archie said, grimacing at the sound. "What the hell are they shooting at us? A fucking cannon, for Chrissake?"

"Whooee!" Blue exclaimed. "That's a coupla big ol' machine guns, buddy. And them fellers know how to use 'em!"

"Archie!"

The scout looked over at the direction his name was shouted from. "Yeah?"

"The Falcon wants to see you," Paulo Garcia yelled at him.

"Oh, boy!" Archie said under his breath. "Now I get to run through them big slugs!" He braced himself, then leaped out of the cover and ran across a short but exposed expanse of ground. NVA bullets kicked up splashes of mud at his heels as he raced to safety. Archie dove behind the other truck where Falconi and Swift Elk had situated themselves.

"You called, sir?"

"Yeah," Falconi said. "We've got to get the hell out of here."

"Oh, I agree with you on that point, sir," Archie said. "In fact, if you was to take a vote—"

"Knock off the bullshit," Swift Elk snapped.

Archie nodded and gave the commanding officer his full and undivided attention.

"That section of NVA riflemen you ran into to the north will be hitting us at any time," Falconi said. "We've got no choice but to go the other way down the

135

river. Check it out and get back here to let me know if we've got a clear run or have to fight our way to safety."

"I'm gone, sir!" Archie said. Without hesitating, he again risked himself in the open while running for the jungle beyond the trucks. He reached the thick brush and immediately disappeared from view.

"I sure hope he finds a way out of here," Swift Elk said.

"If he doesn't—" Falconi let the obvious statement go unspoken.

The enemy heavy machine guns abruptly picked up in volume. The concussion from those Soviet-donated big weapons kicked up dust on the bluff above. The firepower was so overwhelming that not one of the Black Eagles was able to return fire toward the enemy position.

When the volume of slugs died down, the noise was exchanged for that of shouting men. Thinking that the Americans were demoralized by the sweeping fire of the Soviet heavy automatic weaponry, the Red commander ordered a quick attack. The NVA rushed down en masse toward Falconi and his men.

Now the Black Eagles were able to return fire. The massed Red infantrymen made excellent targets as the Americans poured a curtain of aimed fire into their midst. The enemy's front rank disintegrated, forcing their buddies in the back to leap over their tumbling bodies.

The defensive volume of fire increased until the NVA attack buckled. A brief hesitation caused them to sustain more casualties until the assault finally disintegrated. They retreated, suffering more dead and wounded, as the Black Eagles continued their accurate,

136

rapid shooting.

"We stopped 'em that time," Top said grimly.

"Yeah," Swift Elk agreed. "But we won't be able to take too much more of that."

"I'll roger that," Top agreed. "Let's hope Archie finds us a way out."

Sporadic fire broke out again, then the DShK machine guns again sprayed their 12.7 millimeter bullets across the Black Eagle position.

Malpractice McCorckel, on the extreme right flank, had his concentration broken by a rustle of vegetation near him. His first thought was to cut loose with about a half magazine, but he knew that Archie Dobbs was crawling around the bushes nearby. Instead of shooting, he uttered the Black Eagle challenge:

"Calcitra—"

"—Clunis," came back the password in Archie's voice. The scout scrambled inside the perimeter. "Which way to the colonel?"

"Go left," Malpractice answered. Then he quickly turned his attention to returning fire toward the enemy lines.

Archie, on his hands and knees, scurried down the positions until he found his commanding officer. "Sir!" he panted. "I got good news and bad news."

"Give it to me quickly," Falconi said grimly.

"The good news is that I found a way the hell outta here," Archie said.

"And the bad news?" Falconi asked.

"We gotta get out on the NVA side o' the river."

"Damn!" Falconi said. "What's the density of their formations over there?"

"There's a lot of the bastards," Archie answered.

"But we can fight our way through, with luck."

Falconi quickly issued orders to his highest-ranking subordinates Ray Swift Elk and Top Gordon. The battle plan was simple. On command, the entire detachment was to cut loose on full auto, then charge across the river while inserting fresh magazines. Once they were on the other side, they were to move south until contact was broken.

It took the detachment three minutes to be fully prepared.

"Go!" Falconi shouted.

The Black Eagles, nine men on full automatic, cut loose a screen of fire at a combined rate of 1,575 rounds per minute. The flying slugs slapped and slashed into the front NVA positions. The more advanced of the enemy were mowed down in the fighting positions they had chosen for themselves. The awful suddenness and strength of the fusillade swept through them like a huge machete in a bamboo grove.

Falconi led his men into the river. They quickly removed the now empty magazines of their weapons and inserted fully loaded thirty-round clips. Again resorting to the gruesome force of full auto, the first members of the detachment gained the far riverbank.

But the NVA commander was a seasoned veteran. He had expected a strong probe somewhere into his battle position. He didn't know exactly where until that moment. Now he ordered a special reserve rifle section to bolster that point of the line. These dozen infantrymen dashed in to fill the gaps of their dead and dying comrades.

The sudden incoming fire staggered the Black Eagles' progress. Blue Richards, Paulo Garcia, and

Ray Swift Elk had not emerged from the water yet. They struggled desperately through the muddy river as splashes of water splattered them with each NVA bullet that hit around them.

Falconi knew the trio was doomed unless he acted quickly. "Charge!"

The other six men advanced toward the enemy, their fire crisscrossing in the confined space of the jungle trees. This was something the NVA had not expected. The ferocity of the assault forced them to retrace their steps stubbornly, but steadily, backward.

Ray Swift Elk hit dry ground first. He joined the shooting as Blue also escaped the water. The Alabamian turned and grabbed Paulo's outstretched hand, jerking him the rest of the way to the riverbank. The marine grimaced with pain but made no sound. The hand pulled on was the broken one.

"Move left!" Falconi ordered. "Go!"

Archie, wanting to be at the head of the column, damned convention and safety as he rushed forward to gain his usual position.

Within one short minute, the detachment was into the jungle. They followed Archie's frantic trailbreaking as they sought to get out of the battle.

Suddenly the area turned silent.

The Black Eagles slowed down. Top, peering through the overlapping leaves and branches, breathed out in relief, "I think we made it."

Falconi made a quick visual check of his men as they continued on their way deeper into the Vietnamese jungle. Happily, he noted all were present and accounted for. But he wanted to know for sure. He signaled to Malpractice. "Any casualties?"

"No, sir. All hale and hearty," the medical sergeant replied. Then he noticed Paulo's splint. "What happened?"

"Nothing," Paulo said. "Just straighten it up, huh?"

Malpractice examined the injured hand. "Jesus, Paulo! That must hurt like hell." He immediately began work on it. "Somebody really pulled on this mitt o' yours."

"Yeah," Paulo said thinking of the alternative if Blue hadn't grabbed him and pulled him out of the river. "But it was worth it."

Buffalo Soldier Calvin Culpepper was directly to the rear of Archie. He hurried forward and tapped the scout on the shoulder. "You wasn't kidding when you said you'd take us to hell, huh, Archie?"

Archie displayed a grim smile. "Buffalo Soldier, according to my road map, we ain't even close yet."

"Yeah," chimed in Blue Richards behind the two. "I'm beginning to think this mission might get rough."

"Naw!" Archie exclaimed. "Things is gonna stay nice and easy just like they are right now."

"Shit!" Buffalo Soldier said. "If this war ain't bad enough, I gotta get stuck between the two biggest jive-asses in it!"

CHAPTER 12

The "dih-dahs" of the Morse Code beeped in Paulo Garcia's earphones as he tended to his duties as operator of the AN/PRC-47 radio set.

The members of the detachment not on perimeter guard in the jungle clearing watched the Marine as he accurately wrote down the coded five-letter groups that were being broadcast to him from Peterson Field in Saigon.

Finally the sign-off blipped.

Paulo took off the earphones. After ripping the page from his message pad, he took it over to where Lieutenant Colonel Robert Falconi sat with Swift Elk and Top Gordon. "Here you go, sir. The 'latest for the greatest.'"

"Thank you, Paulo," Falconi said, taking the important piece of paper. The Black Eagle commander wasted no time in using a classified deciphering word that would unlock the complicated code. He copied the message down onto a special preprinted grid, placing each letter into its proper space. Only the detachment commander, the executive officer, and the sergeant major were privy to this ultrasecret puzzle-solver.

Falconi labored over the project, creating what appeared to be a complicated crossword puzzle. It took him nearly fifteen minutes to unravel the message that SOG headquarters had sent them. After the work was complete, he stared at it.

"Shit!"

"Bad news, sir?" Top asked.

"Kind of," Falconi replied. He gestured to Swift Elk. "Let's have a command conference."

The words were a hint to any lower-ranking Black Eagle within earshot to withdraw immediately. Blue Richards and Paulo Garcia found something to do out on the perimeter.

Swift Elk waited until the men had made themselves scarce. "What's the word from SOG?" the Sioux asked as he settled down with the CO and topkick.

"We've got orders to withdraw immediately from the AO," Falconi said. "They want coordinates of a convenient LZ before daylight tomorrow."

"Hell, we just got here," Top said, shaking his head in puzzlement. "What the hell do they want us out of here for? We ain't fucked up the mission yet."

"Right!" Swift Elk echoed. "I'd say we're doing damned good. We just dumped almost an entire NVA company into a river, didn't we?"

142

"We sure as hell did," Falconi agreed.

"And we've disrupted a VC supply route to the point the sonofabitches are nervous as nuns in a whorehouse about using it, haven't we?" Top added.

Falconi decided to play the devil's advocate. "Yeah. But there must be some reason—maybe even a *sound* one—for SOG to want us out of here."

"Did they give any particular rationality?"

Falconi shrugged. "Nope. The message is pretty simple. He handed it to Swift Elk.

Swift Elk read the words while Top peered over his shoulder:

ULYSSES TO EAGLE. WITHDRAW IM-
MEDIATELY REPEAT WITHDRAW IM-
MEDIATELY FROM AO. PROMPT COM-
PLIANCE IMPERATIVE. SEND MAP CO-
ORDINATES FOR NEAREST CONVENIENT
LZ PRIOR TO DAYLIGHT TOMORROW.
CHINOOK WILL MAKE PICK-UP OF DE-
TACHMENT. REPEAT PROMPT COMPLI-
ANCE IMPERATIVE. OUT.

"I'd say they want us to skidaddle away from here pretty damned quick," Swift Elk said.

"So it appears," Falconi said thoughtfully. "But do you know what my first reaction is?"

Top chuckled. "Yes, sir. You want to tell 'em to shove them orders, right?"

"Right," Falconi said. "I'm sick and tired of getting hassled by those bastards back at headquarters."

"Usually they're shoving our noses into the shit," Swift Elk said. "I wonder what's behind this sudden tender loving care on their part."

"Maybe a pushy, big shot general wants to send in a pet outfit of his own to grab some glory," Falconi suggested. "That wouldn't be the first time something like that happened. Some brass hat will send in a bunch of guys he doesn't like to do the initial and most dangerous groundwork, then let some of his fair-haired boys come in to mop up and grab the glory."

"I think you're right," Top replied. "Like the lieutenant here said. It never bothered them to stick it to us in the past. So why the sudden concern?"

"You don't suppose that headquarters has suddenly developed a real genuine affection for us, do you?" Swift Elk pondered.

Top shook his head. "Can you think of anything we've done that would make us their sweethearts?"

Swift Elk, remembering the drunken brawls by the Black Eagles in Saigon, smiled. "Nope."

Falconi didn't engage in the good-humored speculation. In fact, he was silent for a long time. The lieutenant colonel remembered the times of being outnumbered, outgunned and out of luck, with no help in sight. The brass had always left it to him and his men to either do-or-die, in the most literal meaning of the cliche. He took a deep breath. "We're staying!"

"Way to go, sir!" Swift Elk said.

"All the way!" Top Gordon said, intoning the old Airborne saying.

Falconi took out his message pad and hastily composed a coded reply to the message. When he finished, the lieutenant colonel glanced out on the perimeter. "Paulo!"

"Yes, sir?"

144

"Crank up the big radio set," Falconi ordered. "I've got a few words to send back to SOG."

"Yes, sir," Paulo said. "Important words?"

Swift Elk laughed. "In essence, the colonel has two words for 'em—and they ain't 'Happy Birthday'!"

Andrea Thuy's fingers flew across the keyboard of the IBM Selectric as she typed out some routine paperwork that was forever flowing across CIA field officer Chuck Fagin's battered old desk.

Her work was interrupted by the buzzer on the office door. She switched on the intercom. "Yes?"

"Verbal message from Gen'ral Taggart, ma'am," came the terse voice of one of the headquarters military police guards.

Andrea pressed the button on the side of her desk. The door popped open, admitting a sharply dressed, severe MP. He properly saluted the woman, who was a lieutenant in the South Vietnamese Army. Andrea returned the military greeting. "What's the message, sergeant?"

The soldier, obviously ill at ease, shuffled his feet in an entirely unmilitary manner. Then he cleared his throat, and spoke out loud and clear.

"The general says for Mr. Fagin to get his goddamned ass up to his office immediately, if not sooner."

Andrea suppressed a smile. "Are those *your* words, sergeant?"

"Oh, no, ma'am!" he protested. "I'd never speak like that in front of a lady—unless I was ordered to. Them's the exact words I was told to use by the general hisself."

"May I relay them, or must you speak personally to Mr. Fagin?"

"The general says you are to tell him, ma'am." He shrugged apologetically. "Sorry, ma'am! Good day, ma'am!" The military police sergeant executed another sharp salute and made a quick but dignified exit.

Andrea waited until the door shut, then she turned and walked directly into the inner office. "Hey!" she said stepping inside.

Chuck Fagin, laboring over an agency report, looked up. "Hey yourself."

"General Taggart says for you to get your ass up to his office immediately, if not sooner," Andrea said.

"That's no way for a lady to talk," Fagin said in mild disapproval.

"Those are the general's precise words," Andrea said. "And that's exactly the way he wanted the message passed on to you."

Fagin sighed. "In that case," he said, "I'd better get my ass up to the general immediately, if not sooner."

"That is what I'd seriously advise you to do," Andrea said. "Do you want me to go with you?"

"If General Taggart didn't specifically invite you, then you wouldn't get inside anyhow," Fagin said. "Wait for me. I'll fill you in later."

"I'll be on pins and needles until you get back," Andrea said.

Fagin got up and shuffled out of the office in his heavy gait. He went through the usual security procedures to get up to the third floor of the building, until he was issued directly and unceremoniously into the general's inner sanctum.

Taggart, staring out a window, whirled and faced the

CIA field officer. "Do you," he demanded, "know what the goddamned word *discipline* means?"

"I think you've asked me that question before," Fagin replied calmly. "What have Falconi and the Black Eagles done now?"

"They've disobeyed—or at least are giving every intention of disobeying—direct orders sent to them through the Special Operations Group communications channel," Taggart said.

"I'm sorry, general," Fagin said. "There is no way I can make sense out of this until you bring me into the big picture."

"The *big picture,* wise-ass," Taggart snarled, "is the fact that a heavy concentration of elite, well-trained, highly motivated, superbly equipped, and competently commanded North Vietnamese troops are moving rapidly into the area of operations where Lieutenant Colonel Robert Falconi and his band of merry pirates are now committed. As much as I hate him and those hooligans he commands, my conscience won't let me allow them their just fate of being slaughtered like stupid cattle. In other words, I want them out of there."

"Well, general, I suggest you promptly order them out," Fagin said.

"I have just told you that they refused that order," Taggart said. He pointed to his desk. "I am going to send that communique sitting there by my pen set. Before it is broadcast, I want you to read it."

"Sure," Fagin said. He walked over and picked up the paper. The CIA officer had absolutely no problem in understanding what the general wanted to say to Falconi.

The words were to the point and could in no way be

misunderstood or misinterpreted:

ULYSSES TO EAGLE. FOLLOW PREVIOUS
EXFILTRATION ORDERS IMMEDIATELY
SAY AGAIN IMMEDIATELY. OPERATION
IS CANCELED. NO MORE RESUPPLY. NO
REINFORCEMENTS. NO NOTHING. FAIL-
URE TO COMPLY LEAVES YOU WITHOUT
SUPPORT. OUT.

"That ought to do it," Fagin said with understatement. "Do you want me to add anything? Or do
anything?"

"No," Taggart said. "But if there are any hearings
about the massacre of Falconi and the Black Eagles, I
want you to be a witness to the fact that they were
ordered to leave the AO. I did not purposely abandon
the crazy bastards out behind enemy lines."

Fagin was worried. "Tell Falconi why he has to
exfiltrate, please."

"Hell, no!" Taggart bellowed. "I don't give anybody
any explanation of orders I issue. My most basic
military philosophy is for my subordinates to simply
lock their heels and say 'Yes, sir!'"

"Falconi is not a regular kind of subordinate," Fagin
protested.

"I'm telling you this plain as hell, Fagin. If Falconi
doesn't obey these orders, he will be on his own. There
will be no support, no communications, no logistical
operations, nothing. *Nothing!*"

Fagin was grim. "There's a good chance Falconi will
stick it out in that operations area, general. And he
won't know or appreciate the overwhelming enemy

forces facing him there."

"Then, Mr. Fagin," Taggart said grimly, "Falconi is fucking dead!"

Paulo Garcia handed off the second coded message received that day. Falconi settled in and went into the drawn-out deciphering process necessary in order to read it. When he finished, he passed it over to Swift Elk. "It looks like there won't be any general's pet unit coming in here, after all. They want us out of here. Evidently this mission is being canceled. At least, that's what I assume."

Swift Elk read the missive and passed it over to Sergeant Major Top Gordon. The Sioux Indian officer wiped at the sweat on his forehead. "I suppose they have a good reason, though. But I doubt if it's just to save our asses. They've probably run out of operational funds."

Falconi nodded. "Yeah. Maybe some rear-echelon finance officer and his staff have worked themselves into a regular snit over money matters."

"Fuck 'em!" Top said.

Falconi lit a cigarette. This time he made no remark about having to quit. Instead, his mind dealt with the situation at hand. There was a strong psychological angle to deal with. The Black Eagle detachment, while always victorious, had gone through several bad maulings during previous operations. The high casualty rate had produced an appearance of dull resignation in the unit, but beneath the combat-weary facade was a hardcore dedication to their unit and the missions assigned to it.

149

Quitting in the middle of an operation seemed like a slap in the face of every Black Eagle who had died in battle.

Falconi, Swift Elk, and Top Gordon fully realized this. Such an action could be demoralizing to the point of destroying the esprit de corps so necessary in an elite unit that drew the most dangerous of assignments.

Falconi continued to smoke in thoughtful silence. Finally, as he reached the decision his mind had been mulling over, he turned to Top Gordon. "Unit formation, sergeant major."

"Yes, sir!"

The men out on the perimeter couldn't believe their ears when the order was passed around to report in to the command post and "fall in."

"Christ!" Archie Dobbs complained. "Is the old man cracking up or what?"

"Yeah," Blue agreed. "He's acting like we was in garrison or something."

"I hope we ain't going to get close-order drill," Gunnar said. "My facing movements are pretty rusty."

"So's your scaly ass!" Top snapped at him. "Move it!" Obviously, neither the commander nor the senior noncommissioned officer were kidding. The detachment was drawn up, each man standing at a rigid position of attention. Top Gordon gave them a quick inspection, then performed a flawless, sharp about-face movement.

"Sir!" he snapped. "The detachment is all present and accounted for."

"At ease," Falconi said. He waited until the men relaxed. Then he launched into a quick report on the order to abandon the mission. When he was certain

150

every man understood the implications of the situation, the lieutenant colonel made a closing statement:

"This is a military organization. As such we operate under the strict discipline demanded of our profession. However, due to the unusual circumstances of this situation and our unit's past record, I feel that whatever decision that is made will be a voluntary one. Therefore, any man who desires to follow SOG headquarters' orders, will be made part of the exfiltration. Those who desire to stay and continue our mission—despite the fact we will be completely on our own—will be allowed to do so." He gestured to Top. "Sergeant major, take over the detachment."

"Yes, sir." Top looked at the men. "We ain't got a lot of time, so I don't want to spend the rest o' the day on this. Just sound off with your decision when your name is called."

The men looked at each other and waited for the unusual procedure to continue.

"Sergeant First Class Culpepper!"

"Hell!" Buffalo Soldier said lazily. "I ain't goin' no place."

"Sergeant First Class McCorckel!"

"I'll stay, sergeant major," Malpractice replied.

"Staff Sergeant Garcia!"

"Marines don't retreat," Paulo stated.

"Sergeant Olson!"

"Vikings don't haul ass neither," Gunnar the Gunner said.

"Petty Officer Richards!"

Blue spat a stream of tobacco juice. "Us Alabamians like to fight."

"PFC Dobbs!"

151

"I ain't chicken," Archie told the top sergeant.

Sergeant Major Top Gordon fought hard to suppress the proud smile that his face wanted so much to display. Instead, he frowned and barked. "Detachment, tinch-hut!" He made another sharp facing movement. "Sir! The detachment enlisted men will all remain."

Falconi nodded. "And so will the officers. Okay then, guys, *calcitra clunis!*"

Buffalo Soldier displayed an easy grin. "I just hope it ain't *our clunis* that gets kicked, sir!"

CHAPTER 13

Once again Archie Dobbs worked as the eyes and ears of the Black Eagle Detachment.

But this time he had company.

Malpractice McCorckel and Gunnar the Gunner Olson moved with Archie through the thick, clinging flora of the jungle that grew so heavily in the operational area. This particular part of the world, except where the NVA and VC had put in trails, was trackless and wild. Thus, Lieutenant Colonel Falconi had figured the presence of the two other Black Eagles would provide enough security for the scout to allow him to apply nothing short of a hundred percent concentration on reconnaissance duties in this remote hell of sylvan Vietnam.

Even with this added precaution, Archie's instincts for tracking were teasing his nerves with vibrations of warning. The territory was isolated and primitive, yet the presence of many humans was evident to such a strong degree that it was antithetical to the environment.

Archie, sweating profusely, finally became so agitated that he signaled a halt.

Malpractice and Gunnar caught up with him. The medic was puzzled. "What the hell? Are you tired or something?"

"No," Archie said nervously wiping at the sweat trickling down his face. "I hate to admit it, guys, but I'm getting a case of the heebie-jeebies."

Gunnar tightened his grip on his M16 and cautiously glanced around. "Do you figure there's some NVA or VC close by?"

Archie almost sneered. "Hell, yes, Gunnar! Who do you think we're gonna run into out here? The Lennon Sisters, for Chrissake?"

"Fuck you, Archie!" Gunnar snapped back at the sarcasm.

"Yeah? Well, fuck you too, Gunnar!"

"Hey!" Malpractice said. "You two dickheads keep it down. You want to draw the whole Communist world down on our asses?" He nudged Archie. "And you lighten up, Prince Charming. What's the problem anyhow?"

"The problem, sergeant, is that things ain't adding up," Archie said. "This was supposed to be an isolated supply area used only as a place for passing through to the regular combat territories, right?"

"They said there was some camps," Gunnar said.

"Even whores, remember?"

"Yeah," Archie agreed. "But they'd be few and far between. I swear that ever' hunnerd meters or so, I see a footprint or some bent grass or snapped twigs where somebody has passed by. This place is crowded, man!"

"That's kinda hard to believe," Gunnar said. "It's so godawful wild around here."

"No matter the scenery, we'll have to be more careful," Malpractice said. "But remember that Falconi sent us out here on a recon mission, not to sit around and discuss the concentration of the local population."

"Okay," Archie said. "Let's get on with it, then." He glanced over at Gunnar. "Sorry for snapping at you like that, Swede."

"That's okay," Gunnar said. "If you don't call me 'Swede' no more. I'm Norwegian."

Archie shook his head. "It'd sound stupid to call you 'Nor,' so now I'm apologizing for growling at you and also for calling you a Swede."

"Okay. We call ourselves 'Norskis,'" Gunnar said with a grin. "Anyhow, you can always make amends by buying me a cold beer."

Archie smiled back. "Fuck you, Gunnar."

Gunnar gave him a friendly pat on the shoulder. "Fuck you too, Archie."

With the air cleared between the two Black Eagles, the patrol got on with its assignment.

The rate of travel was slow, but steady. After only a half hour, Arcie held up his hand for another intermission in the activities. He motioned his partners forward. He answered their quizzical expressions with a tersely whispered, "It's another goddamned trail! This place must be criss-crossed with the things."

Malpractice went past Archie a few paces. He could easily see the well-worn track that cut a two-meter wide swath through the trees. He added his own description to Archie's report: "A *well-used* trail!"

"I got a suggestion, guys," Gunnar said. "Since the damned thing looks like it's a VC answer to Broadway, what do you say we squat down here and see who's using it?"

"Sounds good to me," Malpractice announced. "From the appearance of the ground, it seems the traffic along here is kinda heavy." As the senior ranking man in the patrol, his casual comment was as good as a direct order. "Let's situate ourselves so we can't be seen though."

The Black Eagles were already pretty well camouflaged. Between the black and green patterned tiger fatigues and the brown and green stripes of camo grease on their exposed skin, they could melt well into the surrounding brush with near invisibility. Exercising noise discipline, they each found a good hiding spot that gave them excellent views of the trail passing in front of them.

Then it was more of the hurry-up-and-wait crap that was so prevalent in Black Eagle operations.

An incredibly slow seventy minutes dragged by. The surrounding jungle seemed to accept the three men as natural additions to the environment. Animal and insect activity, which had died off dramatically at their arrival in the area, gradually picked up until it was back to normal. A breeze, high in the tree tops, made the limbs of the taller trees sway back and forth a bit.

"I wish some o' that breeze could reach us," Archie said while feeling the growing itch of the heat rash irritating his crotch.

"Shhh!" Malpractice hissed.

Archie sighed and went back to observing the open track that ran past them. Gunnar almost nodded off to sleep, but he suddenly popped wide awake when the distant sound of human voices disturbed them.

The noise grew gradually louder until a group of a half dozen Viet Cong came into view. Each of them had an empty carrying pack slung across his shoulders.

"Porters," Malpractice whispered lightly.

Although they carried no visual loads on their backs, they seemed to be tired. But, despite their fatigue, they moved quickly out of sight.

"What do you make o' that?" Archie asked, after the strange procession had passed out of sight and hearing.

"Yeah!" Gunnar said. "They're all wore out, but they ain't carrying nothing."

Malpractice, the wise old sergeant, knew the answer. "That's on account o' they've already delivered their loads."

"Then what's their hurry?" Archie asked. "Them guys are walking as fast as a second lieutenant going to a comp'ny commander's meeting."

"Because," Malpractice said patiently, "they're on their way to get more of whatever it is they're toting around. That's the only logical answer."

Archie became excited. "That means a depot down the trail somewheres."

"You bet!" Gunnar agreed.

"That pretty well cuts our work out for us. Let's go find it," Malpractice said. "Lead on, Archie."

Archie, in his professional opinion, considered speed necessary enough to sacrifice a bit of security. He took

157

the patrol out onto the trail itself and led his buddies on a relatively fast-paced trek up to a point where a widening of the jungle track showed they were closing in on a central location of some kind.

There, the three Black Eagles slipped silently back into the jungle.

In less than a quarter of an hour they were situated at the edge of a large clearing. Wide-eyed and surprised, they looked out onto a small military garrison complete with billets, storage huts, and even a small parade ground. Archie summed up the find in one excited word:

"Depot!"

Malpractice smiled grimly. "That's what we've been looking for, guys. Archie, mark this baby on your map. We don't want to make any stupid mistakes and lose it."

"I'm way ahead o' you, Malpractice," Archie said, putting a barely discernible pinpoint on his topographical chart. This almost unseen marking was necessary. In case of Archie's death or capture, any enemy intelligence officer scanning the map would not know what the Black Eagle had been up to or particularly interested in. "When we get a little farther away, I'll shoot an azimuth and confirm this location." He thought a moment. "I'll make a sketch of the camp layout, too. That ought to come in handy. It's risky, but Falconi is gonna have to know ever' inch o' this place."

"Right," Malpractice said. "C'mon. Let's get back to Falconi and the others. It won't be long until we pay this place a more conspicuous visit."

Then Gunnar the Gunner Olson sighted the most exciting aspect of the entire camp. "Look! Women!"

158

A group of young Asian females loitered outside a large thatched building. From their shouted banter with the passing NVA and VC troops, it was obvious they were neither schoolmarms nor nurses.

Andrea Thuy stirred the frying vegetables in the wok, then spooned them out into a serving bowl. "Come and get it, ladies," she called out.

Betty Lou Pemberton and Jean McCorckel wasted no time in seating themselves at the small dining table. They had been invited by Andrea for a late dinner in her Saigon apartment. The women all shared one common, uniting detail of their lives: their men were members of the Black Eagle detachment.

Andrea and Robert Falconi had become lovers at the inception of the outfit. She was not only an officer in the South Vietnamese Army, but her childhood in the northern regions of French Indochina made her a valuable intelligence asset to the detachment. For that reason she had been attached to the unit and had even participated in several combat operations with it. But her passion for Falconi changed her status from "valued contact" to "risky liability," and the young Eurasian woman born of a French father and a Vietnamese mother had been transferred to office work as Chuck Fagin's administrative assistant.

Second Lieutenant Betty Lou Pemberton's contact with Archie Dobbs had begun when the feisty scout had been medically evacuated back to the U.S. Army hospital at Long Binh where she was stationed as an army nurse. During Black Eagle Operation Cambodia Kill Zone, Archie had taken an incredible fall from an altitude of thirteen thousand feet while a malfunctioning parachute strung out behind him. Anyone else would have been killed by the drop, but Archie had survived somehow with Malpractice McCorckel's ministrations. To add to the implausibility of the situation, the scout had recovered quickly from his injuries. During this time, he and Betty Lou fell in love. Her affection for the brave Black Eagle was so great that she had actually aided him in going AWOL from the hospital to rejoin the detachment in the field.

Jean McCorckel, on the other hand, was solidly and happily married to her particular Black Eagle. She and Malpractice had met during Black Eagle Operation Song Cai Duel, when she had served as his nurse in the dispensary in her native village of Tam Nuroc. They had gone through hell together, taking care of the wounded and dying under fire from attacking NVA troops, while growing closer emotionally. When the operation ended, Malpractice was granted an administrative leave. Rather than spend it in the fleshpots of Tokyo or Hong Kong, the medical sergeant returned to Tam Nuroc to claim the woman he loved. They were quickly married and traveled to Saigon, where Jean, as a registered nurse, got a job on the same hospital ward with Betty Lou. She and Malpractice rented an apartment not too far from Andrea's.

Now, as the dishes were passed around, Jean spooned out a helping of rice onto her plate. As she passed the plate to Betty Lou, the young Vietnamese woman glanced over at Andrea, who was their only source of information on their men. "You are sure you have heard nothing?"

Andrea shook her head. "Only that a resupply drop

160

had been requested," she said. She knew, of course, of the hassle about getting the detachment back in from the field. But the top-secret classification of Black Eagle business prevented her from telling the other women the truth of the situation. Andrea forced herself to display a reassuring smile. "There's nothing to worry about, girls."

"I hope not," Betty Lou said, cutting her portion of the pork roast that was the main dish. "Archie is so unpredictable and rash that I'm afraid he'll do something—" she hesitated, then laughed lightly and added, "—stupid!"

Jean, who had seen plenty of war in her lifetime, patted her friend's arm. "Sometimes being foolish is a good way to survive in battle. As for myself, I worry about Malcomb because he is so unselfish. He will risk his own life to help his friends."

Andrea thought of Falconi. "That man of mine certainly is no shrinking violet in firefights. And I ought to know. I've been in combat with him."

"I just wish this terrible war would end so we could all get on with our lives and stop worrying about the men we love getting killed," Betty Lou said sadly.

"That is something I have never considered," Jean said. "In my years there has always been fighting. First the Japanese, then the Viet Minh, and now the Viet Cong and the North Vietnamese. To tell you the truth, I have never considered the possibility of peace."

"It *is* possible," Betty Lou assured her. "And I'm sure it will come about someday."

"In the meantime," Andrea said, "we worry."

"Let's talk about something else," Betty Lou said. "Andrea has already calmed our ragged nerves with her assurances that everything is fine."

"Yes," Andrea agreed. "Let us talk of other things."

The three women settled into forced joviality as they made themselves create a light atmosphere at the strained dinner.

Robert Falconi pointed to the sketch map that Archie Dobbs had put the finishing touches on only minutes previously. "This," he said, "is the target for tomorrow night."

The other eight Black Eagles looked at the paper. "What's the mission, sir?" Lieutenant Ray Swift Elk asked.

"Stated simply—attack, loot, retreat," Falconi said.

"How is the execution phase going to be run, sir?" Paulo Garcia asked.

"We'll make a daylight move to the target area," Falconi answered. "Obviously, noise discipline is going to have to be of prime importance. We'll go slow, with plenty of flank and frontal recon to make sure the NVA don't spring any surprises of their own. Upon arrival at the target site, we'll go into position here—" the lieutenant colonel indicated a spot on Archie's drawing, "—we'll cool it until dusk and make a silent penetration into the depot proper."

Buffalo Soldier Culpepper raised his hand. "I reckon that'll include quiet killing, as well."

"Right," Falconi said. "Swift Elk, Top, and Archie will take out any sentry posts in the way, and open a path for us. Once we're inside, we'll go directly to the storage area for weapons and ammo. If we're lucky, we'll be able to sneak back out. If not, we'll blast our way back to the jungle. The bastards, even if they wake up and catch us, should be surprised enough to be a bit flat-footed for a few precious minutes."

"Those will be minutes," Top announced, "that we will take full advantage of."

"Exactly, sergeant major," Falconi agreed. "Okay, men, tomorrow is going to be a long, long day. Let's set up perimeter security and catch some Z's before first call tomorrow."

"I don't want to argue with you, sir," Blue Richards said lazily, "but if we're lucky, tomorrow will be a long, long day. If we ain't, it's gonna be a short, short day for a few of us."

"Well, on that happy note, I bid you goodnight," Falconi said.

Top cut things short. "All right! First relief, move out on post. Go! The war starts again tomorrow."

CHAPTER 14

The waning sunlight of early evening shone through the thick tree canopy of the jungle in shafts of weak illumination.

Three NVA infantrymen were loitering behind the sandbags of their picket post in the dull light. Since they anticipated their reliefs from outlying guard duty at any moment, the soldiers relaxed while chattering and smoking their cheap Chinese cigarettes. Hot rice and fried fish awaited them back in the garrison. Having not eaten since early morning, they looked forward to the coming meal. After that, they would give the joy girls in the rustic garrison some consideration.

But the Black Eagles in the brush had other plans

for them.

"Go!" Top whispered softly.

He moved forward through the gloom with Swift Elk and Archie beside him. Their approach to the enemy position was masked by the NVA's careless conduct. The Red soldiers' eyes were turned toward the direction of their camp, eagerly watching for the approach of the new shift of guards.

Each Black Eagle, as silent as a stalking puma, glided over the shallow parapets of the picket post. Their arms simultaneously locked around the NVA's necks while, at that same exact instant, their K-bars were thrust upward with every ounce of physical strength they could muster. The sharp blades sliced through flesh and muscle in an instant, the steel entering just under the bottom ribs and biting into vital organs.

A brief struggle ensued. Bloody bile was coughed up by the dying North Vietnamese, and was vomited into the American hands covering their mouths. Finally the shuddering stopped and the bodies were gently and quietly lowered to the ground.

Top turned and signaled back to the rest of the detachment. Within seconds, Falconi led the other five men forward. The lieutenant colonel glanced down at the trio of dead NVA. "They went quick and quiet. Nice work."

Archie wiped the filth off his hand on one of the sandbags stacked around the post. "Thanks a lot, sir. Yeech!"

"We promised you adventure when you enlisted," Falconi said. "But we didn't say it would be clean." He glanced through the overhanging trees to the darkening sky above. "It'll be dark in another ten minutes.

166

We'd better move into our attack position now."

Top Gordon formed the men up as a line of skirmishers. "Stay alert," he urged them. "Now move forward—slowly!"

Obeying their senior noncommissioned officer, the men kept their M16s ready as they neared the Communist camp. Swift Elk had positioned himself in the center of the formation. The natural warlike tendencies that he had inherited from his Plains Indian ancestors heated up his blood and caused him to walk a bit faster than the others.

That was the exact reason he bumped into the guard relief first.

The North Vietnamese, expecting nothing more than seeing their buddies at the picket post, were totally unprepared for confronting any hostile individuals in the jungle—particularly a vicious one sporting his camouflage face paint in the streaked war patterns of the Sioux Indian nation.

Shocked, they stood stock-still for a split second.

Nine M16s cut loose, the explosive spray of bullets splattering into the trio. They were cut down into bloody sacks of human debris. This quick, decisive action wiped out any chance of surprise the Black Eagles had. Falconi's dedicated, hardcore mind knew only one course of action to follow in such an explosively dangerous situation.

"Charge!"

The line surged forward, picking up speed as they charged into the camp. But the momentum of the assault was quickly broken up by an obstacle that had remained unseen until that moment. Whoever commanded the garrison believed in secondary lines of defense. The evidence of this military philosophy became frighteningly apparent when the Soviet DShK heavy machine gun opened up.

For the second time in that mission, Falconi and his Black Eagles faced death from this formidable Russian automatic weapon.

The slugs, many of them sizzling tracers, zapped through the air around Falconi's men. They went down as the line of fire gradually lowered. Falconi looked desperately around for a quick way out of the deadly circumstances. His unit was pinned down, and it would be only a matter of a very short time until flanking attacks would seal their doom.

But Blue Richards was on the extreme right of the skirmish line. If Swift Elk had inherited fighting tendencies from his ancestors, then so had Blue, from a family descended from Confederate soldiers. Although unable to shout a proper Rebel yell, the quick-thinking navy Seal rolled farther out until he was free from the incoming volleys of machine gun slugs. Then, pulling a grenade from his patrol harness, the Alabamian crept forward until he was within throwing range of the NVA position. A quick look showed him the peril of his buddies' situation. Blue grasped the grenade in his right hand and slipped the pull-ring of the pin over the muzzle of his rifle. A quick yank pulled the restraining device free, and he let the spoon pop off.

"One! Two! Three! Four!" he counted in a whisper to himself.

Blue hurled the grenade and dropped to the ground. It hit a yard short of the target but took a healthy bounce forward, then rolled straight into the machine gun nest. The explosion kicked the big weapon over and shredded flesh from the crew.

"C'mon, y'all!" Blue yelled, standing up. "Let's hit them sumbitches while the hittin's good!"

The detachment instantly responded to the entreaty, and again surged forward into the interior of the camp. But, after only a dozen steps, they were again forced down, this time by some wild but rapid shooting from a trench.

This time it was Paulo Garcia's turn to take the spotlight. He signaled to Archie nearby. "Cover me!"

"Go for it!" Archie yelled. He opened fire on the enemy position.

Paulo leaped up and ran a few paces forward to some cover offered by a stack of crates. He stopped there and swung his rifle into action. Paying no attention to the pain in his injured hand, the marine cut loose with short, accurate bursts of automatic fire.

Now it was Archie's opportunity to advance. He scurried forward to a fallen log adjacent to Paulo's crates. When he reached it, the scout flung himself down and resumed spraying his volleys at the NVAs in the trench.

Paulo noted that the enemy were keeping their heads down. "C'mon, Archie! Let's wrap it up!"

Now, as a two-man assault team, the pair both charged, firing deadly salvos of 5.56 millimeter bullets. When they reached the edge of the trench, they hosed it without mercy.

Four NVA collapsed under the onslaught, but another three made an attempt to escape. The two Black Eagles cut them down before they could reach the end of the defensive ditch.

Now they took advantage of the fighting site.

Rushing to the opposite side, Paulo and Archie showered the rest of the camp with their crisscrossing patterns of semi- and full-automatic rifle fire.

The rest of the detachment, now able to move freely behind this covering fire, advanced rapidly and joined them in the trench. Sergeant Major Top Gordon wasted no time in placing the men in the best positions for maintaining the volleys into the enemy-occupied section of the garrison.

"Brace yourselves!" Falconi yelled out. "They'll be coming this way." The Black Eagle commander expected an enemy counterattack, but he knew it would be quickly conceived and carelessly carried out at this stage of the battle. "Set a couple of grenades in front of you," he ordered.

The men carefully removed two grenades from each of their harnesses. Blue, on the other hand, had only one left after knocking out the machine gun nest.

Falconi's silent prediction came true. Within three minutes a wild, yelling assault was launched from the opposite end of the camp.

"Get a grenade and pull the pin!" Falconi yelled.

The attacking NVA, receiving no initial fire, were encouraged. They quickly stepped up their pace, until they were running full tilt toward the Black Eagles.

"Get ready!" Falconi hollered. "Throw!"

Nine grenades lobbed up and out in lazy arcs. The attackers barely noticed them until the objects kicked up some dust when they bounced on the ground. The very front NVA suddenly realized the significance of the items. They desperately turned and attempted to run back. But their comrades behind were coming too fast and hard. The collision in the Red line would have been comical if the grenades hadn't suddenly exploded.

Shrieks of pain from the wounded sounded but were quickly smothered by the roaring of Black Eagle M16s. The attack melted into piles of green-uniformed figures of maimed and dead men.

"Go! Go!" Falconi ordered. He leaped out of the trench and ran toward the buildings on the far side of the garrison. His men were not going to be left behind. They scrambled after him, jumping over the fallen victims of the enemy attack.

Fire-and-Maneuver became the name of the game. The Black Eagles leapfrogged in a pattern of covering each other and advancing as they closed in relentlessly on the last remnants of resistance left in the camp.

The final defenders had barricaded themselves in the garrison's only solidly built building. Unfortunately for the NVA, this was only a structure of two-by-fours covered with thin planking.

Certainly not the type of fortification to keep out bullets.

"Everybody!" Falconi ordered. "On full automatic. I want each man to empty no less than three magazines into that place."

The din that followed was deafening, and it lasted for a full minute. Almost a thousand rounds blasted the flimsy edifice, turning it into such a hunk of Swiss cheese that one side fully collapsed to the ground.

"Cease fire!" Falcon bellowed. "Move in and mop her up."

The men went forward cautiously, ready for any traps or survivors so dedicated they would be willing to trade their lives for someone else's. But the assault had been complete. The interior of the splintered structure revealed only the bloodied corpses of dead North Vietnamese soldiers and a few Viet Cong guerrillas.

"Archie!" Top called out. "You and Blue run a quick recon on the edge of the jungle there. Be careful. There might be a sniper or two."

"Right, sergeant major," Archie said. "Let's go, Blue."

"I'm with you, good buddy," Blue answered, hurrying over to join the other Black Eagle.

The remainder of the detachment made a thorough search of the camp. Appropriately, it was Gunnar the Gunner Olson who found the camp armory. He went inside and emerged carrying a Soviet RPK light machine gun. "Look what I found!"

Falconi and the others grinned at the man who loved automatic weapons. The lieutenant colonel had an idea. "I'll tell you what, Gunnar. I've checked my roster and found there's an opening for a crack gunner. Want the job?"

"Do I carry this baby, sir?" Gunnar asked.

"Is it heavy?" Falconi asked.

"Prob'ly not more'n a dozen pounds," Gunnar said. "And there's seventy-five-round drum magazines in here for it."

Top was interested. He walked up and checked out the weapon. "It says on the receiver that it's 7.62 millimeter."

"Good," Falconi said, joining them. "That means it'll use the same ammo as the AK47s."

"What AK47s?" Swift Elk asked, approaching.

"The ones we're trading these M16s for," Falconi answered. "From this point on, we'll be toting the same weaponry as the NVA and VC. That means they'll also

172

be our source of supply."

"Great idea," Swift Elk said enthusiastically. "Especially since our own side won't give us logistical support."

"That's exactly why we're going to be carrying weapons the enemy will surely have bullets for," Falconi explained.

Top started to say something, but he glanced past the commanding officer at a sight that made him wide-open in surprise. "For the love of God!"

Archie and Blue, with a half-dozen young Asian women, stepped out of the jungle and walked across the garrison toward them.

Buffalo Soldier Culpepper stared intently at the unexpected females. "What the hell you got there, boys?"

Archie grinned. "Me and Blue can always be counted on to use our good looks to scare up some broads."

"You get some pretty scary ones all right," Malpractice said. The women were not too good-looking.

Paulo Garcia, as male as anyone in the detachment, had a different interest in them, however. As an intelligence man, his professional curiosity was aroused. A few terse, to-the-point questions got him the information he needed. He turned to Falconi. "These are 'joy-girls' for the VC, sir. They're the backbone of any R&R the Commies have for their troops."

"Lucky bastards," Gunnar Olson said, forgetting his newly acquired machine gun. He gave the girls a close look. "On the other hand, they ain't gonna win no Miss Southeast Asia contests, are they?"

Falconi looked around at his troops. "I hope none of

you Romeos have any romantic plans for these unfortunate young women. Their lives are miserable enough without our adding any more to the depression."

The women, obviously frightened, instinctively huddled together under the gaze of the large, strange men who stared at them.

Falconi displayed a kindly smile. *"Chao co,"* he greeted them. Then he continued in their language. "Do not be afraid. We will not harm you. One of my men must ask you questions about the soldiers you serve. Then we will take some guns and bullets and go away." He motioned to Paulo. "Get to work, intelligence sergeant."

"Aye, aye, sir," Paulo said. Adopting his commander's attitude, he escorted the women to one side of the garrison and sat them down. After passing out some chocolate candy from his C-rations, he launched into a gentle, but persistent interrogation.

In the meantime, the other Black Eagles began breaking up their M16 rifles. The remnants were thrown into a bonfire that Archie built. After this was done, Gunnar passed out confiscated AK47s and bandoleers of the 7.62 millimeter ammunition to serve them. When every man was equipped, Sergeant Major Top Gordon conducted a thorough inspection to make sure no one was lacking in combat preparedness. He turned to Falconi. "Sir," Top announced, "we're a hunnerd percent ready."

"Fine, sergeant major," Falconi said. "Let's move 'em out of here, then."

Top motioned to the detachment. "C'mon, you bunch o' pirates! You want to live forever?"

The Black Eagles moved out. Blue Richards looked back at the joy-girls who, obviously relieved, watched the foreigners leave. "So long, darlin's," the Alabamian said. "We're gonna miss you."

"I ain't gonna miss 'em," Buffalo Soldier said. "If you look up the word 'ugly' in the dictionary, you're gonna see their pictures, man!"

CHAPTER 15

Brigadier General John Taggart trembled with rage. Pale-faced, he roared at Fagin, "Don't you talk to me like that, you Irish bastard!"

Fagin, as furious as the general, bellowed back, "You'd damned well better make sure any supply drops requested by the Black Eagles are taken care of PDQ! You're getting goddamned close to what could be considered criminal conduct, Taggart!"

The two enraged men stood shouting at each other across Taggart's desk.

"You don't come into my office and make demands, you sonofabitch! And you don't discuss the legality of my official decisions, either," Taggart said. "You're getting as high-handed and out-of-control as those goddamned Black Eagles. The situation is clear enough for even a thickheaded idiot like you to understand, Fagin. The goddamned NVA are going to saturate the operational area like a holiday crowd at Coney Island. If Falconi and his bandits don't get the hell out of there, they are going to be up to their necks in NVA and VC. We have taken the appropriate steps by ordering them to exfiltrate immediately. The Black Eagles, on the other hand, have come across with their usual damn-your-eyes attitude, and chose not to obey those lawful, direct orders."

"The bottom line—" Fagin started to say.

"The *bottom line* is that Falconi has committed the ultimate fuck-up," Taggart interrupted. "This time he has displayed the worst judgment possible—he has brought about the death and destruction of himself and his command." The general displayed a sarcastic grin. "Custer would be proud of him."

"All you have to do, Taggart, is tell him what the situation is," Fagin argued. "He and his men are not the type who accept the 'obey-to-the-death' philosophy. They have to understand the situation to react to it."

"What the hell's the matter with just doing as they are told?" Taggart demanded.

"You know why, Taggart," Fagin hissed. "You and other brass hats here at SOG have socked it to those guys more than once. You've sent 'em into situations worse than this one, for Chrissake!"

"Well, Fagin, maybe I'm trying to make amends," Taggart said.

"Give 'em the word, Taggart," Fagin insisted. "Explain things to 'em."

"I am a brigadier general in the United States

Army," Taggart said. "When I issue an order, I do not explain it to anyone except my lawfully appointed superior officers. My method of conducting military business is to have my fucking subordinates lock their heels and say, 'Yes, sir,' then run out to obey my goddamned orders immediately, if not sooner!"

"Then let me contact Falconi," Fagin said. "I'll put him in the big picture and your sensitive feelings won't get trampled on."

"It would still be the same thing," Taggart said. "And I'm getting sick and tired of talking about this. There will be no further action unless Falconi radios in for exfiltration. Now get out of here!"

"Hey!" Fagin shouted. "Hey! You don't dismiss me like that, asshole!"

There was one moment of stunned silence as the general stared in indignant disbelief at the man across from him. The officer walked around his desk, his voice strangely calm. "What did you call me, Fagin?"

"I called you," Fagin said patiently, "an asshole."

Taggart smiled and brought a bolo punch straight up from the floor. His fist smacked Fagin under the chin. The CIA man's head snapped back and he walked backward for three steps. Then he shook his head and grimaced. Now he smiled.

Then he charged.

Fagin's assault brought him back into the range of Taggart's fist. The general, an ex-enlisted man who'd done his share of barracks room brawling before going to West Point, was damned good. His punches were crisp and telling, popping off Fagin's face like a pair of miniature jackhammers.

Fagin, wising up, counterpunched and danced back

179

to break contact. He began bobbing and weaving, working his way forward while staying wary of Taggart's expertise in fistfighting. When Fagin was close enough, he made a superb fake of launching a right hook, then pivoted slightly on his left foot and delivered a lightning-quick *mawashi geri* kick.

Taggart's superb training and instincts saved him as he performed a faultless *gedan barai* parry that blocked the kick. "Hey, Fagin. No karate, okay?"

"Okay," Fagin panted, making a gentleman's agreement. He bobbed and weaved a couple of times. He went into his next movement, which was a right hook that wasn't a feint.

It connected.

Taggart spun toward the wall and barely avoided a painful collision. When he turned back, Fagin was on him, dragging him down to the ground. The general, being twenty pounds lighter than the CIA officer, had a hell of a time breaking free. When he did, he rolled away and quickly regained his feet.

Now the two stubborn men were literally toe-to-toe, trading punches as their faces began to dissolve into bloody messes. Two full minutes of this mutual punishment continued until the door burst open and a pair of brawny MPs burst into the room with Andrea Thuy behind them.

It took a few anxious moments before the combatants were separated. Finally, with each held tightly by an MP, they stared at each other.

Andrea shook her head. "The Black Eagles are out there fighting for their lives, and you two idiots are in here acting like schoolboys!" But she realized that a sort of male bonding and masculine understanding had been reached between the pair of brawlers.

Taggart snapped his head in her direction and treated the young Eurasian woman to an angry glare. Then he looked back at Fagin, and relaxed. "Let me go, soldier!"

"Yes, sir," the MP said.

The general motioned to the other G. I. "Release Mr. Fagin," he ordered.

Fagin was turned loose. He wiped at the blood dripping freely from his nose. "Shit! Whew! You throw a hell of a punch, Taggart."

"Fagin, I'll make one compromise," Taggart said. "I'll grant your request about radioing Falconi."

Fagin's battered features broke into a happy grin. "Thanks, Taggart."

"But!" the general cautioned him. "There will be no support of any kind. Only an exfiltration as ordered in the original broadcast to them."

"I appreciate that, really," Fagin said sincerely.

"I'll reiterate," Taggart said. "Exfiltration only! If Falconi wants to die, he'll refuse it."

Fagin, with Andrea's help, walked out of the office and headed for the elevator. Andrea held on to him. "When are you going to raise the Black Eagles?"

"To quote the general—'immediately, if not sooner,'" Fagin answered. "It's either that or Falconi and the guys have had it."

It was late afternoon when Paulo Garcia's AN/ PRC-47 radio beeped to life. The marine carefully recorded the message, then carried it over to Falconi.

The lieutenant colonel, sitting with Swift Elk and

181

Top Gordon, took the page from the message pad. "Maybe the brass has decided to back us, after all," he said, retrieving his decoding book. He began the work of changing the numbers into words. After a few minutes he announced, "This one is from Fagin."

"What the hell does he want?" Top growled.

Swift Elk smiled sardonically. "He probably is asking us to pick up a six-pack of beer for him on the way in from the mission. That way the lazy bastard won't have to leave his air-conditioned office."

Falconi continued the task until he had completed the deciphering. "The word is, guys, that this area is saturated with VC and NVA," Falconi said. "He's advising us to obey the orders to bug out."

"Fuck him," Top said.

"And the horse he rode in on," Swift Elk added. "Hell, we know we're up to our eyeballs in the bastards."

"Anyhow," Falconi said. "The matter has already been decided within the detachment in a democratic fashion." He began writing an answer, then called Paulo Garcia over. He handed his communication to the marine. "Send this back directly to Chuck Fagin."

"Aye, aye, sir," Paulo answered. He went to his radio and set the transmitter key into action:

EAGLE TO IRISH. WE STAY SAY AGAIN WE STAY. THERE IS A JOB TO DO WHETHER WE HAVE SUPPORT OR NOT. THE BLACK EAGLE DETACHMENT WILL HOLD THE LINE HERE UNTIL RELIEVED OR WIPED OUT. SAY AGAIN UNTIL RELIEVED OR WIPED OUT.

When Paulo was finished, he reported back. "It's done, sir."

"Fine," Falconi said. "Now let's stop fucking around and get back to work on those NVA papers we found at the depot."

"Yes, sir," Paulo answered. He pulled a sheaf of documents out of his large side pants pocket. "I been through these, colonel. Most of 'em are routine admin stuff." He grinned. "I guess the North Vietnamese Army has got the same paperwork bullshit we do, huh?"

"Yeah," Falconi agreed with an amused smile.

Top laughed out loud. "I always had a real strong suspicion that there was one guy in this world—just one single, solitary sonofabitch—who was hired by ever' army just to create paperwork. I bet he's got an office at the North Pole where he does nothing but send out reports and correspondence that creates tons of administrative chores."

"Sounds like an adjutant's Santa Claus," Swift Elk said.

"No matter," Paulo said. "But now and then something real interesting pops up. Like this." He handed a manila envelope to Falconi. "Inside here is a directive that is asking for supply reports. It says these logistic summaries are to be sent directly to General Trong at a place identified as Camp Cau Nay Co."

"Very interesting," Falconi mused. "Do you have any idea where this place might be?"

"You bet, sir," Paulo said. "I used one of their maps to check it out. After comparing it with our own, I found it's located about fifty kilometers from here."

Top raised his eyebrows in curiosity and surprise.

"Sir, do you have any special interest in this here General Trong?"

Falconi nodded. "Damned right, Top. We're going to kill the sonofabitch!"

There was a section of Saigon that was unique even for that exotic city. Although not an actual political department or zone, it had its own name: *Le Quartier des Colons*.

Here were the voluntary expatriates of metropolitan France. Members of their country's foreign service, many had once left Indochina to go back to France but they had discovered that after years in the colonial service, they were strangers too far removed from old customs and traditions to become regular Frenchmen again. They were *colons*—colonials—now and forever.

These individuals lived in the past, in a time of colonial grandeur and authority, when they were the rulers of this humid, hot land. Most of them were only a step or two above poverty. In fact, the ones that were the best off were the retired bureaucrats living on their pensions. The rest had minor jobs in the South Vietnamese government or ran their own businesses— none too lucrative.

Andrea Thuy lived in the *Quartier des Colons*. She loved the atmosphere and the quaint little sidewalk cafes that were shabby imitations of those in Paris. Her apartment, had it not been for the air conditioning and other trappings necessary in a tropical climate, would have looked as though it had been plucked right out of the *Berge Gauche*.

Fagin, his face clearly showing the effects of the fight with Taggart, sat in the cab with Andrea beside him.

The woman suppressed a smile. "I have to admit that was the most amazing sight I've ever seen," she said. "You and Taggart—"

"Knock it off!" Fagin snapped.

"All right, Chuck," she said. "But—"

"*But,* hell! I'm your boss, goddamnit! Now shut up about that fight," he said. Fagin settled into sullen silence for a few moments before he spoke again. "I was just about to really stomp his ass when those frigging MPs busted in on us."

Andrea laughed out loud, immediately covering her mouth. "I'm sorry!"

"Change the subject," Fagin ordered.

"Okay. Now tell me why you accompanied me home," Andrea said.

"I ain't taking you home," Fagin said. "I just want to see somebody that lives near you." Suddenly he leaned forward and tapped the Vietnamese driver on the shoulder. *"Durng lai!"*

The cabbie obediently pulled to the curb and stopped. After Fagin paid the fare, he and Andrea stepped out onto the sidewalk. "I'll see you later, Andrea."

"Aren't you coming up?" she asked. "You know I always keep a fifth of Irish for you."

"It's tempting," Fagin said, walking away. "Give me a rain check." He waved and hurried down the street until he reached a bar called Le Bar du Loiret. It was a shabby, down-at-the-heels place. Fagin went inside, going directly to the bartender. "Is Raoul here?"

The man answered with a curt nod of his head toward the rear of the place.

Fagin hurried back and found a customer asleep with his head down on one of the cheap tables. He grabbed the guy's hair and pulled him up to look at his face. "Hey, Raoul!"

Raoul Luellette's eyes slowly opened to half-mast. Finally he recognized the man who was handling him with such indignity. "Ah! 'ello, Fagin, *mon ami,*" he said in a slurred voice.

"Listen to me, you drunken Frenchman," Fagin whispered so he wouldn't be overheard. "Can you still fly a Dakota?"

Raoul licked his dry lips. "Buy me a *vin rouge,* Fagin. *S'il vous plaît!*"

"Answer my question, goddamnit!" Fagin repeated himself. "Can you still fly a Dakota?"

"Do you 'ave one, *mon ami?*"

"I know where I can get my hands on one o' them babies," Fagin responded.

"Then I can fly it," Raoul said. He changed the subject "Please, Fagin, buy me a drink—a red wine, that is all I ask."

"No way," Fagin said. "I have a job for you, and you're gonna have to be dry to pull it off." He slipped his arm under the Frenchman's and hauled him to his feet. "C'mon!" He propelled the unresisting man toward the door.

"Where do we go, *mon ami?*"

"Raoul, my friend," Fagin said. "I'm taking you on a *grand aventure*—a big adventure. Lots of excitement and danger, you'll love it!"

"*Oui?* It sounds like I could get killed," Raoul said as he was taken out onto the street."

"Well, old friend, if it's any consolation to you, we'll get killed together," Fagin said. "Now move along now. We don't have a hell of a lot of time."

186

CHAPTER 16

The tread of the sentry's rubber-soled boots crunched on the gravel strewn thickly across the garrison yard. This portion of the military complex surrounded the miniature villa in the center of the compound.

Archie Dobbs crouched in the darkness, watching the guard make his rounds. The gravel was alien to this primitive jungle environment, and the Black Eagle scout knew it had been brought in for two reasons:

(1) To dress up the joint. This was a sure indication that a general officer was stationed there; and,

(2) For security. It was impossible to walk on the stuff without making noise.

The guard reached the end of his post and stopped. He swung his AK47, worn at sling arms, from across his shoulder to a position of "high port." Then he smartly executed an about-face, and retraced his steps back across the gravel. This exaggerated parade ground maneuver was another indication that there was a brass hat in the vicinity.

Archie could easily have taken the man out, but that wouldn't have been wise at that point in the proceedings. It would be better, the scout reasoned, to wait for the man's relief. That way there would be more time available for deadly mischief before any more of the sentries made an appearance.

Archie's point of observation was near one of the posts of the barbed wire fence that surrounded the Vietnamese army post. There was plenty of room for him to slide into the garrison proper, and enough shadows to offer concealment. He stayed in this waiting place for three-quarters of an hour.

The Black Eagle scout's presence at that particular point and space in time was not only because of his usual job assignment in the detachment. This particular duty had much more involved in it than a simple area reconnaissance. Falconi knew that a high-ranking North Vietnamese general was in that garrison. There was no need for any sneaking-and-peeking to verify that. What the commander wanted was for that particular general to be dispatched to that great headquarters in the sky. Or, as Archie himself so aptly put it, "to be wasted."

Naturally, such an operation required a bit more than skillful scouting. Stealth and the ability to move quietly and remain unseen came into play as well. Because of Archie's multitalents in these various deadly crafts, it was logical for him to perform the task of assassination. After all, he was inarguably the best recon guy among all the Black Eagles. Then another study in logic came into the picture when it was necessary to pick the man to actually "waste" the general. To send someone else in with Archie would be to risk two lives in the dangerous undertaking. Therefore, Lieutenant Colonel Robert Falconi decided to minimize the jeopardy to his small command by having the same man who found the best way in do the entire job alone.

Thus, Private First Class Archie Dobbs was chosen to administer the *coup de grace* to Major General Trong of the People's Army of North Vietnam.

Now, still waiting for the changing of the guard, Archie's mind wandered occasionally to Betty Lou, or to how nice a cold beer would taste. Then his attention would snap back to the present.

His thoughts were dwelling on his sweetheart when a flurry of activity interrupted his romantic reverie. The steady cadence of marching feet approached. Then a trio of NVA troops marched into view from around the villa. Two were privates and a third sported collar-rank badges of corporal. The guard whom Archie had been watching leaped into the position of attention and faced them.

The three marched up and halted. After a brief exchange, one of the privates stepped out of the small foramtion and the guard took his place. Then they all marched off, leaving the new sentry alone.

This was the one Archie had to kill.

This fresh trooper immediately began marching back and forth across his proper post with the same drill-field snappiness of his predecessor. From his appearance, one would think he was on parade in front of Ho Chi Minh himself. Each pace was a measured goose step, and his free arm swung in the Russian style, while the other held the AK47 rifle sling in the correct manner.

Archie, much less elegant but a hell of a lot quieter, slipped under the barbed wire and slow-crawled to the deeper shadows afforded by a tall rung tree. This was the farthest point of the guard's little parade. When Archie reached the place, he set his weapon down and silently slid his knife from its sheath on his boot.

Then he waited.

The guard walked up to the usual stopping point. He halted, then performed a smooth, faultless about-face. He stood stock-still for an instant—the same instant that Archie Dobbs eased up behind him and clamped a strong, clenching hand across the man's nose and mouth. The knife blade slipped through the uniform jacket and continued on through flesh, under the lower rib and up into the kidneys. The damage was instantaneous and massive. The victim's struggles only intensified the bleeding and hurried his death.

Archie carefully dragged the body to the other side of the tree and gently laid it down. After resheathing the knife and retrieving his rifle, the Black Eagle crept slowly and carefully across the gravel, until he gained the steps leading to the villa's porch. He ascended the short stairs and strode through the open door that seemed to beckon him to enter.

The building was weakly lit by small kerosene lanterns in holders mounted to the wall. A dim, flickering illumination showed Archie the way down a long narrow corridor. He noticed a couple of rooms along the way, but there was no evidence of any particular activity.

Suddenly a door at the far end opened and a decidedly feminine figure stepped out into the hall.

Archie pressed back against the nearest door and worked the knob in suppressed panic, afraid he might make some noise and attract the woman's attention down to him. The portal opened a bit, and Archie slipped into the dark room on the other side. He kept the door opened a crack and peered outside. The woman passed by, and even in a brief glimpse, he could see how extraordinarily beautiful she was. Archie smiled to himself. Now he knew which room the general slept in. A good-looking whore like that called for more money than any NVA enlisted man could afford.

Suddenly a wild snore startled the Black Eagle.

Now, with his eyes used to the dark, Archie could make out the figure of a sleeping man on a bed in the room. The guy snorted again, then rolled over and dropped back into deep, rhythmic breathing. Archie snuck back out into the hall and waited a breathless moment to make sure he was alone. Satisfied, he proceeded down toward the door from which the woman had emerged.

Archie hesitated only long enough to take a calming, deep breath before entering the room. The chamber was dimly lit by a small electric lamp. The place was obviously the quarters of a ranking officer. A fancy, western-type bed and dresser dominated the furniture in the place. Unfortunately, there was no one on the rumpled sheets. The flushing of a toilet in the next room caught Archie's attention.

A short, bandy-legged Vietnamese in silk pajamas stepped out into the bedroom. Archie wasted no time in drawing his knife and rushing the man. The general did not hesitate, either. He made a quick move toward some clothing on a chair and retrieved an automatic pistol.

Archie reached up and grabbed the officer's wrist and stabbed at him. But General Trong now had locked a tight grip on Archie's own arm. They struggled in gasping, grunting silence, each pushing and shoving to gain enough advantage to bring his own particular weapon into play.

Archie pulled back slowly and steadily with his knife hand, taking advantage of his own height. Trong worked in the opposite way. His pistol-gripping hand was above Archie, and he was working hard at bringing the barrel down far enough to put a bullet in the American's head.

Sweat broke out on the grimacing faces of the combatants as each grappled in cold, growing rage. There were no thoughts between them about anything else except the destruction of the other.

Suddenly Archie's hand broke loose and he made a wide, clumsy attack. The knife bit deep into the side of the general's body, making hot blood pour out. The officer gasped and instinctively squeezed the pistol's trigger. The loud report of the weapon was deafening in the room.

Archie struck again—again—and a final time before the tough NVA general sank to his knees. He looked up into Archie's face and snarled a garbled, incomprehensible curse before pitching face first onto the carpeted floor.

Archie pivoted on his heel and raced toward the door. He burst through it and ran down the hall. But before he could reach the porch, a Vietnamese soldier appeared. Archie brought up his AK47 and squeezed off a long fireburst. The man bent over from the jar of a half-dozen rounds slamming into his midsection before collapsing.

Archie hit the porch and leaped over the cadaver. The gravel crunched under his own boots and those of an NVA squad as he raced for the fence.

A floodlight blazed to life and bathed the area in a brilliant yellow glare at the same instant that Archie dived under the fence and rolled into the jungle.

The NVA riflemen, close enough to make out the intruder's features, all cut loose simultaneously, sending a half-dozen sprays of 7.62 millimeter slugs flying toward the Black Eagle attempting to escape.

Chuck Fagin and Raoul Luellette stood under the lamp mounted over the military warehouse door. A nervous South Vietnamese army lieutenant paced back and forth in front of them. Finally he turned and faced the CIA man and his French companion.

"This is most irregular, Mr. Fagin!"

"Not at all," Fagin said, adopting a reassuring tone. He pulled some documents from inside his jacket pocket. "These are official requisitions—quite legal."

"I have had only a cursory glance at them," the lieutenant said. "And I must insist that you allow me a closer examination."

"Of course," Fagin said. He handed the papers over to the man.

The lieutenant looked them over. "These are official."

"They certainly are," Fagin said.

"But they bear no signatures," the ARVN officer pointed out.

"Not now," Fagin said. "But when I am in receipt of the required material, I will gladly sign."

"That won't be enough," the lieutenant said. "The logistics chief must also put his name to them."

"Lieutenant," Fagin said calmly. "You know who I am, do you not?"

"I have known you for two years, Mr. Fagin," the officer replied. "You are an officer in the American Central Intelligence Agency."

"That is correct," Fagin said. "Therefore, would I do anything improper?"

"I do not know—"

"Will my signature alone suffice?"

"I am not—"

"If it does not, you may certainly make a legal case out of this," Fagin said. He pointed to Luellette. "And I have a former officer of the French Air Force with me, too."

Further conversation was interrupted by the arrival of a two-and-a-half ton truck complete with a work crew of ARVN soldiers. The men dismounted from the vehicle and awaited instructions.

"Okay," Fagin said. "Here's what we need to haul out of here." He looked at the requisition and began reading, "C-rations, five cases; 7.62 millimeter ammunition, ten cases; three dozen M26 hand grenades; and four light cargo parachutes with containers."

The soldiers immediately went to work. Within

twenty minutes the entire load had been carried out of the warehouse and was securely loaded aboard the truck. "That's it," Fagin said. He turned to the lieutenant. "Thank you very much."

"Don't forget to sign the requisition, please," the officer reminded him.

"Certainly," Fagin said. He quickly signed, then led Luellette over to his jeep. When both were seated Fagin signaled to the truck driver. "Let's go."

The South Vietnamese lieutenant watched them drive away. He looked at the requisition, then suddenly yelled out and ran after the departing vehicles. "Mr. Fagin! Mr. Fagin! Please! You signed the name Peter Rabbit to these requisitions! Mr. Fagin!"

Archie, fleeing for his life, made no effort to return fire at his pursuers. He leaped up after rolling under the wire and renewed his flight for freedom.

The North Vietnamese guards, desperate to kill the interloper, charged up to the fence. It was the last thing they ever did.

The Black Eagle detachment, concealed at the edge of the jungle, blasted a full-automatic volley into their ranks. Barbed wire broke, fence posts splintered, and the NVA soldiers were blown away in the storm of steel.

"Pull back!" Falconi ordered.

The men withdrew from their positions and followed a trail of luminous tape they had put up prior to Archie's entrance into the compound. It took them less than five minutes to cross the stretch of jungle to the road on the other side.

Then the situation deteriorated.

An NVA motorized patrol, alerted by the shooting, had moved into position to cover their predetermined area of security responsibility. When the commander of this small unit saw the shadowy figures of men come out onto the road, he ordered the spotlights on his vehicles turned on and trained on them.

The reaction to the illumination was instantaneous and instinctive. The Black Eagles wheeled toward the glares—each side toward its own particular field of fire—and blasted them out.

But that didn't discourage the NVA. They fired blindly, hoping like hell to hit something in the inky darkness. But Falconi had already led his men across the road and into the relative safety of the jungle.

But as they left this present danger, each man now fully realized that their stubborn refusal to obey the order to exfiltrate from the mission had left them stranded in the middle of swarming, numerically superior enemy forces, with no easy or clear way out.

As Blue Richards was to say later that same day, "Boys, we're like the coon in a pack o' hounds. They's only one way out, and that's straight up. But, boys, neither us or that ol' coon got wings!"

CHAPTER 17

The NVA outfits stationed in and around Camp Cau Nay Co were first-rate veteran combat units.

Although the assassination of General Trong was not discovered for more than an hour after Archie Dobbs's undignified exit under the barbed wire fence, the enemy subordinate commanders on the battalion and company levels had already launched an all-out offensive against the Black Eagles.

This lightning-quick reaction was not a stroke of luck on the part of the North Vietnamese majors and captains. It was the result of effective prior planning and disposition of troops.

After the encounter with the motorized patrol and its spotlights, the Black Eagles continued their attempt to break contact with the enemy units. But the growing activity in the area surrounding them gave grim notice that a major effort was underway to intercept and destroy them.

Twenty minutes after the retrograde movement had begun, the flares appeared overhead.

The light from these illumination devices did not fully penetrate the dense jungle, but they cast enough brightness to make visibility relatively easy in the battle area. In the beginning, this helped the Black Eagles by permitting them to step up the pace of their withdrawal.

But, unfortunately, it also made it easier for the NVAs in the jungle to spring an ambush on them.

The rush of incoming fire swept across the detachment, forcing everyone immediately to hit the dirt. Within an agonizingly short five seconds, the Black Eagles were pinned tight to the ground by the horrendous, thunderous rush of incoming automatic fire.

A disconcerted, uncoordinated effort was made by several individuals to withdraw from the fiery hell being poured into them. But the Communist soldiers knew exactly what they were doing. They had sealed up all avenues of escape with crisscrossing patterns of offensive fire.

But the one thing the enemy hadn't counted on was a very pissed-off Norwegian-American named Gunnar the Gunner Olson. The young Minnesotan's Viking blood grew hotter with each salvo that slapped in and around the Black Eagles' unplanned battle position. Finally, after carefully timing the pattern of NVA fire, Gunnar made his move. He quickly rose up on one knee and swung the bore of the Soviet RPK light machine gun, emptying the entire contents of a seventy-five-round drum in tightly controlled hosing actions.

No less than a half dozen of the Red troopers crumpled under Gunnar's deadly skill with his favorite type of weapon. Lieutenant Colonel Robert Falconi, stationed to his man's right front, correctly and instantly surmised what was happening. He quickly realized that a brief, temporary superiority of fire had been achieved by Gunnar's brave action.

"Shit and git!" he yelled out in his unmistakable loud voice.

The detachment wasted no time in leaping up and bugging out deeper into the jungle along their original path of withdrawal. Gunnar slammed a fresh drum into the weapon and followed. When a few scattered assault rifle shots kicked up behind him, he whirled and gave the bastards another taste of hot steel-jacketed slugs. The NVA ducked again, and the Black Eagles successfully broke contact.

The next twenty minutes was a cursing, stumbling trek through thick vines and over large, twisted roots of jungle trees. All this was done in a combination of light and darkness as the persistent NVA kept the flares flying overhead. Archie Dobbs led this race for freedom and safety, instinctively following his unerring talent for faultlessly maintaining a desired direction.

Archie kept his keen eyesight and depth perception in top form. Long before any other member of the detachment realized it, he had discerned a break in the jungle vegetation ahead. Only when he slowed down did the others know that something undiscovered lay ahead. Finally Archie halted and signaled the others to hit the dirt.

Falconi, of course, moved up forward. "What's caught your attention, Archie?"

"There's an open area ahead, sir," Archie said. "I don't know what it is, but I'll go forward and check it out."

"I'll keep you company," Falconi said.

The two moved forward another dozen meters. The flares, still zipping across the night sky, provided dim illumination. But it was enough to show a road.

"The last time we saw something like this we were hit by spotlights," Faloni said. "Run a recon up and down here. If everything is all right, we'll move across and into the jungle on the other side."

"Right." Archie went up to the road and listened for a few moments. Then he took a couple of careful glances. After that, he stepped out onto the road and slowly traveled up and down, sticking close to the jungle. Within fifteen minutes he was back with the detachment commander. "Looks okay to me, sir."

"Right," Falconi said.

They returned to the detachment and sought out Sergeant Major Top Gordon. Falconi, wishing he could light a cigarette, gave his orders. "There's a road to cross ahead. You know the drill."

"Yes, sir," Top said. "And so do the men."

Within short moments, the senior noncommissioned officer had the entire detachment lined up at the edge of the jungle, facing outward. After physically checking every man, he gave the order: "Go!"

They all rushed across at once. This method offered a minimal time to be within the rifle sights of any enemy. In less than a couple of heartbeats, they were back into the safety of the jungle, invisible to any observers.

Malpractice McCorckel, however, had been on the extreme left flank of the Black Eagle formation. As he ran into the treeline, he turned his head for a brief glance to his side of the skirmish line. He spotted a solitary NVA for an instant. But the Red ducked away. Malpractice wasted no time in getting to Falconi with the news.

"There was just one guy?" Falconi asked.

"Yes, sir," Malpractice answered. "And he scrambled away."

Swift Elk, standing nearby, volunteered his own impression of the situation. "He's probably a scout, sir. No doubt he's headed back to get the rest of his guys to come after us."

Falconi grinned. "You figure he's the North Vietnamese answer to Archie Dobbs, huh?"

"Yeah," Swift Elk said. "Except Archie would have taken a shot before he hauled ass."

"Okay," Falconi said. "Then we'll get the hell out of here before that guys brings up his buddies."

Once more, with Archie in the lead, the Black Eagles sought a way out of the flood of NVA saturating the immediate area. For the next five minutes the impromptu route was still dimly but adequately marked by the ever buzzing NVA flares.

Then the jungle turned utterly, totally, and unfathomably black!

"Hold it!" Archie whispered back. "Ever'body down!"

Unable to see, the scout needed a respite in order to get his bearings and continue on at a much slower pace.

201

There was a dreadful silence as the inky peril seemed to penetrate through their jungle fatigues and seep into the Black Eagles' souls.

Crump!

"What the fuck was that?" somebody asked.

"Oh, shit," another whispered. "Mortars!"

A whirring whistle sounded, then an explosion some twenty-five meters away erupted, sending a millisecond of brilliancy across the scene. The men went down so fast and hard that their jacket buttons were pressed into the jungle mud.

"I'll change my evaluation, sir," Swift Elk said to Falconi. "That NVA that Malpractice saw wasn't a scout. He was a goddamned forward observer for a mortar battery."

Crump!

"Shit!"

Another deafening detonation roared outward for a brief second. The whirring of speeding sharpness whistled overhead.

Crump!

The shell was definitely closer. And this time the shrapnel didn't fly off through the air. It slapped into the surrounding trees, sending thousands of pieces of splinters whirring through the area.

Top's voice was flat and unemotional. "They got our range."

Falconi was also aware of the situation. A couple more shells, and the detachment would be pulpy hunks of flesh splattered and pounded into the soft earth. "That battery is to our direct front!" he yelled out.

Crump!

"Go get 'em—now!"

202

The Black Eagles rose up and charged forward. The incoming round slammed into the ground to their immediate rear. The concussion from its explosion sucked the air from their lungs. Quickly recovering, and yelling at the tops of their voices, they surged forward through the jungle. The growing fulminations of the mortar shells provided the light they needed to see where they were going.

A few dozen meters ahead of the Black Eagles, the North Vietnamese mortarmen labored at their tubes. The gunners, now that the range was known, relaxed from the sights and watched their assistants serve the weapons. Shell after shell was dropped into the weapons, always firing with a deep, loud *crump!*

The battery commander continued to talk to the forward observer, urging the man to move closer to the target area to see what devastation was being rained down on the invaders. Now and then he glanced up to make sure the mortar crews were working efficiently and effectively in firing their weapons. But the final time he raised his eyes brought him the last sight he would ever see in that particular lifetime.

A tall man with black skin burst out from the jungle. The man, howling like an enraged tiger, pointed an AK47 toward the enemy commander and pulled the trigger. The officer caught a bullet in the throat. The slug exited the rear of his skull, taking a large hunk of brain and his entire tongue with it.

The rest of the battery, their personal weapons neatly stacked to the rear, hesitated at this unexpected sight of their intended targets actually charging them. The sweeping fire that sliced through their formations was fiercely efficient in its killing potential.

Within seconds every NVA mortarman was down, either dead or wounded. Falconi didn't take the time to revel in the victory. "Move on out of here," he ordered. But he yelled out at Buffalo Soldier and Blue, "You two guys, make sure those mortars won't be fired at us again."

"Yes, sir!"

The pair waited until the rest of the detachment cleared the area. Then they rapidly tossed grenades into the stacks of shells around the enemy weapons. They turned and ran, reaching the safety of the trees at the same time that the jungle shook and rocked under dozens of explosions that were so close together they seemed as one gigantic detonation.

Palm fronds drifted down from above while dust and debris were whipped and kicked through the air. Misdirected shrapnel either sailed off into the inky sky or further mutilated the NVA mortarmen lying scattered through the battery area.

Buffalo Soldier and Blue walked back to the site of the former mortar battery. "That," said Blue, "is what I call a real boom-boom."

"Yeah," Buffalo Soldier agreed. "Now let's get back with the detachment. We ain't outta this shit yet."

Falconi continued to lead his men through the enemy-saturated area in search of a way out. They managed to move for an unhindered half hour before Archie again signaled a halt. As usual, Falconi went forward to see what was happening.

Dawn had begun to break, and a pale, rosy light made visibility relatively easy. Archie waited for Falconi to join him. Then, grinning, he pointed through the trees to an open area. "I found something

204

that might be useful to us, sir," he announced. "An NVA motor pool."

Falconi went to the edge of the jungle. A small cleared space was filled with various makes of Russian vehicles. These ran the gamut from small scout cars to the larger GAZ-63 cargo trucks. There were a few soldiers at sentry posts, and one machine gun position beside an entry road.

Falconi was thoughtful for several short moments before he announced, "We're going for a ride." He motioned to Archie and led him back to the rest of the detachment.

Experienced combat veterans faced with a situation that demands immediate and effective decisions are always at their best. Falconi had already formed his plan of action by the time he called his men to an impromptu briefing. Within thirty seconds of his closing remarks, all had moved into position and were waiting the signal to begin the attack.

Falconi opened the ceremonies with a long burst from his AK47.

The Black Eagles moved forward as skirmishers. Well-aimed sprays of 7.62 millimeter fire swept back and forth across the area, with Gunnar the Gunner's light machine gun playing a deadly backup chorus. Blue and Buffalo Soldier, in their usual roles, lobbed two grenades that sailed over three rows of vehicles and landed with deadly accuracy in the machine gun nest by the entrance to the motor pool.

The NVA gunners, in response to the roaring hell sweeping in on them, had just begun the process of turning the barrel of their DShK heavy weapon when the grenades exploded. Shards of shrapnel and two belches of concussion kicked both them and the machine gun over.

Paulo Garcia leaped into the nearest truck and leaned under the dashboard to hot wire it. After kicking the engine to life, he leaned out the door. "Let's go!"

Falconi urged his command to leap into the back of the big vehicle, then he joined Paulo in the cab.

"Which way, sir?" the marine asked.

"North is as good a direction as any," Falconi said.

"Aye, aye, sir!" Paulo pressed down on the accelerator and drove the truck toward the entrance. They rolled past the dead NVA machine gunners and hit the main road. Paulo turned the wheel to the right, and they sped off away from the enemy garrison.

CHAPTER 18

A heavy, sullen silence lay over the Black Eagle encampment, with the same morale-draining discomfort caused by the heat and humidity.

The escape truck, which had been destroyed and abandoned, was a hunk of twisted, scorched junk on melted rubber tires. It was more than five kilometers away, a distance Falconi and his men had traveled by hacking their way through the jungle.

A perimeter had been set up, and a period of rest and waiting was begun. With rations and ammunition short, and the men exhausted after more than twenty-four hours without sleep, this respite in the war had been a vital necessity. Falconi's command post, no more than a small, cleared space in the center of the camp, was crowded with him, Swift Elk, and Sergeant Major Top Gordon.

Falconi lit a cigarette. "I guess it won't make much difference if I give these up or not now."

"Prob'ly not, sir," Top said. He took a deep breath and slowly emitted a long sigh. "This mission is dead," he said with a tone of finality and logical acceptance. "I ain't complaining. That's just a fact."

"I'll tell you another fact," Swift Elk said. "There is no way out of here. I'd say we're right smack between 'that old rock and the hard place,' as the saying goes."

"No escape," Top said, summing up the Sioux Indian's statement.

"We also need supplies," Falconi added. "The NVA and VC are really going to be on the prod now. I'm sure they've found the general that Archie wasted. They won't let up an instant until they wipe us out."

"Or do something worse," Top said. "Like capturing some of the guys and putting them on trial as war criminals."

Falconi emitted a sardonic laugh. "That Archie looks like a criminal no matter what he does."

"He is most definitely not good public relations," Swift Elk said. "Even under the best of circumstances."

"I wonder how the guys are facing up to all this," Top remarked. "We've had some damned terrible times before, but they've been quick and explosive, with plenty of action. Whatever would have happened to us would have been fast and furious. This situation is going to be dragged out, I'm afraid. There's going to be some time for deep and forlorn thinking."

"There's one damned good way to check morale," Falconi said. "Let's go talk to those magnificent

208

bastards and see what's on their minds."

The three highest-ranking Black Eagles picked up their weapons and walked slowly out onto the defensive perimeter. Archie Dobbs, hearing them approach his position, nodded a greeting. "Jesus! All three of you. I must really be in trouble this time."

"No," Falconi said. "We're just running a check on the defensive set-up. Pretty quiet out in the jungle, huh?"

"Except for my rumbling stomach," Archie said. "I think our next foray ought to be to an NVA mess tent."

"Aside from being hungry and tired, how're you doing?" Falconi asked with a wink.

Archie didn't respond with good humor. "I need some bullets, sir. No shit."

"We'll work on it," Falconi promised. He turned and led his two subordinate leaders to the next position.

Buffalo Soldier licked his dry lips. "Y'all checking on things, or are you here for advice?"

"Advice," Top said. "We're figuring on running up to Hanoi and stealing Uncle Ho's secret plans. Any idea on how to pull it off?"

"Sure," Buffalo Soldier said with a grin. "And we don't have to go to Hanoi for 'em. Just put in a request for 'em at G1 and they'll have three duplicate copies in ever' distribution box in the United States loving Army before tomorrow morning."

"Great idea," Swift Elk said.

"So, aside from working out paperwork problems, how're you doing?" Top asked, kneeling down.

"Good," Buffalo Soldier said. "Except my ears keep listening for chow call and don't hear nothing."

"Right," Falconi said. "Tell me about it."

They left Buffalo Soldier's position and walked a few more meters to where Blue Richards had established himself. The Alabamian came directly to the point. "Anybody got chow? I'm so hongry that my stummick thinks my throat's been cut."

"The NVA will be feeding us," Falconi said. "That means nothing but rice and fish."

"Damn!" Blue said. "You'd think them Commies would know how to rustle up hush-puppies, wouldn't you? Them'd go good with fish and rice. I know. I've et that particular combination back home a few times."

"We'll try to find some cornmeal for you, Blue," Swift Elk said. "You can make your own hush puppies."

"Hang in there," Top said. He gave the navy Seal a wave, then followed Falconi and Swift Elk over to the next position.

Malpractice McCorckel was checking out his medical bag when the trio of senior Black Eagles arrived. He expressed his own concerns for the well-being of the detachment. "How're the guys holding on?"

"They're hungry," Falconi answered. "We're down to our last bites."

"We've got a long way to go before we have to worry about starvation," Malpractice said. "But, unfortunately, Americans don't do well on empty stomachs. We've been spoiled by the good life."

"How's your ammo?" Swift Elk asked.

"Running low, sir," Malpractice said. "But my medical supplies are in good shape."

"Okay," Falconi said. "Hang in there, Malpractice. We've got a long row to hoe before this job is over." He motioned to Swift Elk and Top. "Let's go on down the line."

They found Paulo Garcia gathering up his gear. The marine greeted them with a curt nod of the head. "It's pretty quiet on this side o' the perimeter," he quickly reported. "I'm short on chow and ammo. Right now I've got to get up to the command post and stand radio watch on the AN/PRC-47. Which is a real waste o' time. See ya."

Falconi, Swift Elk, and Top watched him leave. The commanding officer shook his head. "That's one marine that's all business."

The final man on their tour of positions was Gunnar the Gunner Olson. When they reached him, the Minnesotan was applying a thin coat of oil to the outside of his recently acquired Russian machine gun. He was so preoccupied with his task that he instinctively greeted them in Norwegian. *"God dag."*

"Goo-dah to you, too," Falconi said. "I see you're developing a real love affair with that machine gun."

"You bet," Gunnar said. "Me and this beauty are madly in love with each other. I even call her Prinsesse. That's Norwegian for Princess." He made a final wipe with the oily rag he kept in his pocket. "But she's just like any other woman. Prinsesse is starting to complain. She says she needs more ammunition."

"Ain't that just like a woman," Top said. "Give her a jewelry box and she wants jewels to put in it. Prinsesse has a drum magazine, and she wants bullets for it."

"Well," Falconi mused. "We must take care of Prinsesse, huh? In the meantime, Gunnar, you keep her warm."

"Ja sure, sir," Gunnar promised.

When the detachment's hierarchy returned to the

211

command post, they found Paulo feverishly working the dials on the big radio. "I got a contact, sir. It's voice, and it's Fagin!"

Before anyone could say anything, Fagin came on loud and clear. "Eagle, this is Irish. I say again. Eagle, this is Irish. Over."

Falconi wasted no time in grabbing the microphone. "Irish, this is Eagle. Over."

Fagin seemed happy. "Eagle, am I glad to raise you! This is violating every security rule in the book, but I've got to use voice. There's no time for encoding. I am located at Peterson Field, but I have a load for you. I say again. I have a load for you. Rations and ammo and an aircraft to fly it. We are ready for immediate take-off. Over."

Falconi spoke quickly. "Irish, this is Eagle. Sounds great, but we need 7.62 millimeter. We have shit-canned the M16s. Over."

"Roger, Eagle. I figured you had already begun using the enemy for supplies. All ammo is 7.62 and will work wonderfully in Red weaponry. Can you give me coordinates for a Delta-Zulu? Over."

"Negative," Falconi answered. "We're hiding out and not familiar with our location. Is that a problem? Over."

"We can handle it," Fagin came back. "We can make a radio contact with you and get the information during the flight to the operational area. Over."

"Roger," Falconi said. He became practical. "Irish, if you are unable to raise us at that time, abandon the mission. I say again. If we do not respond to your radio, forget it. Over."

"Are things that bad, Eagle? Over."

"Maybe a bit worse," Falconi answered. "But get up in the air and head this way, Irish. We need you. Out." He tossed the microphone to Paulo, and stood up. "Archie! Get your ass over here *now!*"

When Archie hurriedly answered the summons, he found his commanding officer with a map spread out on the ground. Falconi looked up at the scout. "We've got a resupply mission flying in. We need to pick out a drop zone and a safe route to it."

Archie shrugged. "Picking out a drop zone ain't nothing to worry about, sir." Then he ominously added, "But there ain't no safe routes anywhere in this area."

"Then, Archie, we might just get killed trying to get there, mightn't we?"

Archie gulped. "Sir, let me say that I'll pick the *safest* route I can."

Chuck Fagin, Raoul Luellette, and the C-47 Dakota air transport plane they were flying had a lot in common. All were old sweats in the fighting that had been going on for so much time in Southeast Asia.

Fagin's introduction to the long war had been after his military service in Yugoslavia as an O.S.S. agent, and in a slightly more conventional role as a paratroop officer in the 187th Airborne Regimental Combat Team during the Korean War. After that bit of unpleasantness, he had been recruited by some former pals of the O.S.S. into the C.I.A. Since he was already in the Far East, the intelligence agency had thought it best to keep him there. Thus, he began a long stint of duty in Vietnam, Laos, and Cambodia that had eventually evolved into his assignment as the case officer assigned to the Black Eagles.

Raoul Luellette, a bit younger than Fagin, had missed World War II—except as a young boy who had endured a few bombings during the Nazi occupation of France—but he had found plenty of action in French Indochina as a pilot in l'Armée de l'Air. His job in France's air force had been adventurous, despite the fact he'd worked in the transport command. He hauled paratroopers and supplies in and out of countless battles during the fighting going on from 1946 to 1954. The armistice had left him a morose, bitter veteran who took to drink to drown his resentment at what he considered a betrayal of the anti-Communist effort of the French armed forces. The only time he sobered up was during the involuntary periods when Fagin sought him out to do odd jobs as a pilot. These occasional periods of employment gave him enough money to get back to a quiet, prolonged drunkenness that provided him with the hours of forgetfulness he craved.

The old C-47 they flew had also pulled service in that part of the country. First as a member of the same air force in which Raoul served, then, later, as an aircraft for the CIA's Air America. Like the two men in its cockpit, the old Dakota was a grizzled, faded veteran with plenty of heart.

Now, with both engines thundering, these three old soldiers lumbered through the hot, humid sky of Vietnam, bound for a rendezvous with nine of the damnedest fighters who ever sought combat in that unhappy land.

*　　　*　　　*

214

Lieutenant Colonel Robert Falconi spoke into the microphone, giving the precise grid coordinates of the area where he wanted Fagin to deliver the badly needed resupply. He ended the short broadcast with a simple warning:

"Irish, this is Eagle. If we're hit, you bug out and forget us. The enemy is so strong in the area that there'll be no salvaging the situation. Out."

Falconi tossed the mike back to Paulo Garcia. The marine took it and hooked the instrument back onto his radio. He said nothing, the determined expression on his face showing his feelings.

The small column of Black Eagles, following Archie Dobbs, pressed on through the jungle. The ground was soft and yielding, but not so the thorny vegetation they pressed through. Finally, after an hour, they reached easier terrain, finding only palm plants with pliable, giving branches of soft leaves.

Suddenly Archie stopped.

Falconi, like the others, went to the ground. After waiting a couple of minutes, he moved up the column and found the scout. "What's going on?"

"Something's up there, sir," Archie whispered pointing straight ahead.

"I hope it's not a big deal," Falconi said. "That's directly between us and the drop zone we selected."

"Yes, sir. I'll go—"

The NVA attack sprang out of the jungle like an erupting volcano of blasting automatic weaponry. Both Archie and Falconi fell back to the main group. "Spread out and get behind any cover you can!" Falconi ordered. "They're coming straight on at us!"

215

CHAPTER 19

The NVA's battle line swept down onto the Black Eagles' hastily occupied positions. More than a hundred wildly shrieking North Vietnamese infantrymen stormed toward them through the brush.

Gunnar the Gunner Olson, his trigger finger working rhythmically and methodically, stood upright as he hosed streams of bullets from the RPK machine gun.

"Skynd dem, Prinsesse!" he bellowed over the rocking-and-rolling of the Russian weapon.

The front rank of the Reds was splattered and mowed down by these fusillades of automatic fire. But their comrades, coming up from the rear, pressed on.

Falconi was not content with simply shooting down the attackers. He ordered half the men to maintain a curtain of fire to the front while the other half pulled back to better positions. When the second group opened fire, the first took advantage of this covering volley to move under it and rejoin the others. The action was repeated several times, until direct contact with the NVA riflemen was broken.

Swift Elk, breathing hard, was not happy. "We cut ourselves loose, sir. But they'll be up to us soon."

"Right," Falconi said. "So we're going to change things a bit." He looked around for the sergeant major. When he spotted Top, the colonel ordered him over.

"Yes, sir?" Top asked reporting in.

"I want you to take two guys with you. Go back about twenty meters and dig nine hasty camouflaged positions. That'll be one for each of us. And get 'em as deep as you can."

"Right," Top said. "That shouldn't be too hard in this muddy soil." Without asking any questions, the NCO called out two names. "Blue! Buffalo Soldier! Come with me and get them entrenching tools out. Let's go!"

"The rest of you," Falconi hollered. "Get ready. I want to form a line here, and hold it for twenty minutes. Get positioned."

Gunnar set himself up a bit behind the others. That allowed him to employ covering machine gun fire to its fullest. He slapped in a drum and pulled the cocking lever. "This is the last one, Prinsesse. I ain't got no more bullets to give you after this, baby. So be good and give 'em hell."

Swift Elk took the opportunity in the lull to question his commander. "What the hell do you have in mind, sir?"

"We're going to do another fire-and-maneuver to break contact. But this time when we withdraw, every man will get into one of the positions being prepared by Top, Blue, and Buffalo Soldier."

"Good idea, sir," Swift Elk said. "The following attack will find us better positioned to resist."

"We're not going to shoot at 'em when they attack," Falconi said.

Swift Elk was alarmed. "What the hell are you going to do, colonel? Hold 'em off and negotiate with the bastards?"

"Nope. I'll let 'em run right past us."

Now Swift Elk grinned. "Then we become the attackers."

"Right. After they run by, we'll jump out of those positions and hit 'em in the rear."

A sudden rush of gunfire sounded to the front. "Here they come, colonel," Swift Elk said.

"You know," Falconi remarked. "I really hope this works."

Swift Elk had no time for reply other than a look of perplexed astonishment before the battle was again in full swing.

Fagin's eyes roved incessantly between the map spread out across his knees and the terrain he could see through the windshield of the C-47. He pointed to a hump on the horizon, and shouted over the engines' roar. "Line up on that!"

Raoul nodded. "I see it, *mon ami*. The course is three-five-zero. Did I not tell you that a quarter of an 'our past?"

"Yes, you smart-assed Frenchie!" Fagin said. "But I'm still gonna be doing plenty of backseat driving on this trip, whether you like it or not."

Raoul shook his head and double-checked his gyro-compass to make sure he was maintaining the correct course. Fagin leaned over to give the instrument his own inspection. He started to say something when the earphones he wore crackled to life. He answered the call, "This is Irish. Over."

"Irish, this is Tall Guy." The call sign identified the broadcast as coming from Brigadier General Taggart. Fagin sneered, but he said nothing as the message continued. "There is a secondary mission now assigned to Black Eagles. A Special Forces officer is being held prisoner in a Victor Charlie camp in the operational area. It is at the fork of two unnamed creeks. Pick the prisoner up and bring him home. Eagle will set up exfiltration on convenient lima zulu. Over."

Fagin was both happy and unhappy at the same time. The mission, and the importance of getting a Green Beret out of enemy hands, would be enough to make Falconi leave the area of operations. But he wanted to make sure the information was reliable and not the half-assed bragging of some double-agent. "What is the reliability factor of this intelligence, Tall Guy?" he asked. "Over."

"Ten-Ten," came the answer, giving the highest G2 rating. "Go for it. Out."

Fagin immediately pulled his note pad from his pocket and scribbled the information as fully as possible. When he finished, he went back to the equipment bundle in the cargo hold and inserted the

220

orders under one of the holding straps.

The maneuver was a bit more difficult than Falconi had hoped. With three men pulled from his fighting roster, he had to be content with an understrength replay of the previous stratagem for a careful combination of a shielding curtain of aimed shooting with a retrograde movement. The lieutenant colonel, Swift Elk, and Gunnar the Gunner provided the covering fire as Malpractice, Paulo and Archie headed for the rear.

Those three ran past their support fire a few paces, then turned and threw out a curtain of flying steel while the other trio made a run for it.

The play was repeated three times before they finally had traveled back far enough to reach Sergeant Major Top Gordon and his two companions. As the remaining six arrived, the senior noncommissioned officer showed them the fighting holes prepared for them. As each dropped into the shelter, a large palm frond was thrown on top of him. When the final man was concealed, Top dove into his own excavation and pulled the covering vegetation over himself.

In that short space of twenty seconds the entire detachment managed to conceal itself, to silently await the arrival of its pursuers.

When the NVA arrived on the scene, they didn't bluster into the area. These veterans moved rapidly, but carefully, through the entangling jungle, their weapons ready for any sudden appearance or attack by the Americans. The Black Eagles heard the enemies' footsteps around them, then could easily tell the Red infantrymen had passed through their position.

Falconi started the ceremony by suddenly rising up and hosing a wildly swinging AK47 bore at the backs of the North Vietnamese. His burst of fire signaled the others, who followed his deadly example.

These survivors of the suicidal frontal attack were cut to pieces within moments. Gunnar's machine gun worked back and forth, while the other Black Eagle shots were intertwined with his more rapid fusillades.

Suddenly there wasn't an enemy soldier standing.

"Cease fire!" Top bellowed.

The silence pounded on their punished eardrums. Archie climbed out of his fighting hole and walked up to the pile of enemy corpses. "My God!"

Blue joined him. "It was just like that ambush o' them VC at the start o' this mission, huh, Archie?"

"We been kicking ass out here, all right," Archie agreed.

"Let's go," Falconi called out to his men. "We've still got a drop to meet."

Archie, totally confident of the route, stepped out knowing the others would fall in and follow him.

Raoul Luellette worked wheel and rudder pedals to turn the C-47 onto the proper course for the drop. He kept his eye on the gyro-compass as he called out to Fagin. "Prepare yourself to go back there to the bundles, *mon ami!* We are getting close to the drop time, eh?"

"I'm on my way right after I raise Falconi," Fagin said. He pulled the microphone off the instrument panel and pushed the transmit button. "Eagle, this is

222

Irish. Over."

"Irish, this is Eagle," came back Falconi's voice over the earphones. "We're in position and the drop is a go. I say again. The drop is a go. Over."

"Roger, Eagle," Fagin said. "One more item to cover. A new mission has been given you. The orders are in the bundle. Rescue of Special Forces officer from VC. Then you must get him and yourselves outta here. Follow exfiltration procedures in the OPORD. This is no shit. Over."

"Wilco, Irish," Falconi said, showing he was fully ready to obey the new orders. "Come on in and give us our goodies. We're hungry and don't have more than a hundred rounds left between the nine of us. Over."

"Roger. Out," Fagin said. He nudged Raoul and leaned close to his ear. "Take us in. They're waiting for us."

Raoul nodded. *"Mais oui!"* He pushed forward on the control stick to go down to drop altitude, while Fagin struggled toward the back of the airplane.

The C-47 streaked past the small patch of sky visible through the thick trees. The door bundle appeared as did a brief glimpse of Fagin's plump figure, then the aircraft veered off and gained altitude as it flew out of sight.

"Beautiful!" Falconi said as the small cargo chute blossomed outward for the short trip to the ground.

When the equipment slammed into the soft earth of the drop zone, Paulo and Malpractice rushed out to it. They quickly disentangled the parachute from some brush, then dragged the whole load off into the trees.

223

The holding straps were unbuckled and pulled back revealing the stack of rations, ammunition, and grenades that Fagin had brought them. Top found the carefully folded piece of paper that bore the instructions for the secondary mission. He took it over to Falconi. "Here's our next job, sir."

"Thanks, sergeant major," Falconi said. He took the paper and carefully read it. "Lieutenant Swift Elk!" he called out. "It looks like we've got a bit of planning to do."

Swift Elk, who had been supervising the issue of ammunition, joined the commanding officer. "Does it look tricky, sir?"

"Well," Falconi mused. "We've got about forty-eight hours to pull some Green Beret officer out of Viet Cong hands, then hotfoot it to a safe landing zone for exfiltration." He winked at Swift Elk. "Does that sound tricky?"

CHAPTER 20

The trio of Viet Cong sauntered along the narrow jungle path. Their leader, a young corporal, kept the pace brisk as he led his two subordinates away from their camp toward a larger garrison twenty kilometers away.

They had recently received orders transferring them to a unit destined for the fighting farther south. All were excited by this stimulating prospect of going against the hated *My*—the Americans—in battle.

Unfortunately for them, the *My* were closer than they thought.

Falconi, Swift Elk, and Top slipped out onto the trail behind the three guerrillas. In less than a half-dozen long but silent strides, they came up behind the three.

225

Their knives went first into backs, then were drawn viciously across throats and necks to make sure that the enemies' lifeblood was quickly drained.

The bodies were pulled into the brush and dumped unceremoniously into the brush. Top wiped his knife on the thick jungle grass. "Ever' time I do this, I feel dirty," he said under his breath.

"Yeah," Falconi agreed. "But consider the alternative if they'd spotted us and given the alarm."

Swift Elk shoved his knife into its scabbard. "Getting hacked to pieces by machetes is not the way I want to be dispatched to the heavenly hunting grounds."

"C'mon," Falconi said. He signaled to the rest of the waiting detachment, then led them all down the path toward the enemy camp.

A map reconnaissance had been almost laughably easy. The camp, as described in Fagin's hasty handwriting, was indeed situated where two creeks converged and formed a small, single river. The terrain features were so prominent that the Viet Cong might as well have put up a neon sign to announce its location.

The Black Eagles moved fifty meters before melting off into the jungle. The camp, badly guarded, was surrounded by the thick tropical growth, and there was plenty of cover. Falconi and his men settled in for some observation.

The Black Eagles also turned their attention to the food that Fagin had delivered to them. Because of the circumstances in the operational area and the secondary mission assignment, there hadn't been time for them to enjoy a leisurely meal. Now, well hidden, they gingerly opened their C-rations and slowly ate what was available in the cans and packets. Pears, pound cake, beans-and-franks, crackers, and dehydrated fried eggs were among the delicacies consumed by the hungry detachment.

After their hunger was satisfied, half the men were allowed an hour's nap. With plenty of daylight left, the other half would get their snooze time so that all would be relatively refreshed for any night attacks Falconi would want to pull off.

But the main activity of that long afternoon was observation, and the Black Eagles saw plenty in the Viet Cong camp:

The most common events were classes of instruction. Young guerrillas, obviously recruits, received lectures on weapons, tactics, field sanitation, ambushes, and other aspects of the life awaiting them farther south. The students paid strict attention to the instructors, who demanded full cooperation and plenty of old-fashioned recitation in the learn-by-rote method they employed in teaching the peasant boys recruited into the Viet Cong.

There were also the usual camp chores. Falconi made special note of the small garrison's sanitation. This meant that well-schooled officers were in charge of the unit stationed there. A clean area was a disciplined area, and that meant the job of getting the Green Beret prisoner—wherever he was—out of there would not be easy.

Swift Elk, next to Falconi, pointed to one of the classes taking place twenty meters away from them. A VC was standing on a stool in front of a group of his buddies, talking in a loud voice. The expression on his face was one of shame and embarrassment.

"What the hell is going on there?" Swift Elk asked.

Falconi slipped his binoculars to his eyes and observed for a few moments. "I'd say the guy is confessing a bad attitude or some minor crime of breaking camp regulations."

Swift Elk grinned. "Yeah. That's big in the Red armies, isn't it? Can you imagine if we did that? Archie Dobbs would be hoarse from yelling out all his various offenses against the U.S. Army and the human race in general."

Falconi laughed softly, and swung his gaze off to one side. He froze, then spoke rapidly. "Take a gander to the right of the big hut. Tell me what you see."

Swift Elk pulled his own field glasses out of their case and followed Falconi's instructions. A few moments later he said, "I see a crate—not solid, but with slats— wait! It's a cage—maybe for a pig or—" He refocused the binoculars. "Shit, sir! There's a man inside!"

"Right," Falconi said grimly. "And that'll be our Green Beret." He whistled softly. "Top! Get over here. We have some planning to do."

The casual drinkers inside the *Quartier des Colons* Loiret Bar looked up with alarm as a man, obviously enraged, stormed inside.

"Is that sonofabitch Raoul Luellette in here?" Fagin shouted.

The patrons looked at each other, then turned their gazes back on the man who shouted so loud in American English. Finally, the bartender, with a quick nod of his head, indicated the back of the establishment.

"Mucho merci," Fagin fumed in an unintentional combination of Spanish and French. He stormed to the

228

rear and found his quarry fast asleep with his head on a table. "Hey, Raoul! Wake up!" Fagin shouted. "I can't leave you alone for six hours!" He grabbed the pilot by the shoulders and pulled him upright in the chair. "Let's go!"

Raoul Luellette moaned, his eyes again opening to half-mast. *"Quoi*—eh?"

"We still have a job to do, and you've got to be sober," Fagin said, pulling Raoul to his feet. "Jesus! I never should have let you out of my sight."

The bartender, a stocky, swarthy man, stepped out from his workstation. *"Monsieur,"* he said. "You are too much of a bother to my friend, Raoul."

"Fuck off, asshole," Fagin snarled.

"You come in 'ere before and you yell at 'im," the bartender said. "I t'ink you got the bad manners, eh?"

Fagin, displaying a smile of cordiality, exploded a *haisoku* karate kick that went so high that the Irish-American flew over on his back. Raoul, released from Fagin's pudgy grasp, collapsed to the floor with him.

But the kick connected, hitting the bartender straight on the chin. The man's lights went out as he flipped over on his back.

Fagin struggled to his knees. "Damn! I can still do it!" He reached over and grabbed Raoul. "Let's go, asshole!"

The two staggered and struggled across the street to the other side. Pulling and tugging, Fagin got his drunken companion up the narrow avenue to an apartment house. More struggling followed as they mounted the stairs. When they arrived in front of the apartment that Fagin had been looking for, he knocked loudly.

Andrea Thuy, holding her Colt auto .45 pistol, opened the door. She took one look at the two men and displayed an angry frown. "I do't appreciate you bringing your shit-faced buddies up here, Chuck."

"This bastard," Fagin explained out of breath, "is instrumental in getting Falconi and the guys out of the operational area. But I got to get him sober to get the job done."

"Why didn't you say so?" Andrea snapped. She opened the door wide. "Come on in. I'll put on a pot of strong, black coffee."

Archie Dobbs slipped into the VC camp. He moved silently to an empty school shed before stopping to listen. Satisfied that it was at least temporarily safe, he turned back and waved a signal.

Lieutenant Colonel Robert Falconi could easily see the gesture in the moonlight. He crept, catlike, across the short distance and joined the scout. A silent nod, and the two continued their penetration of the Red garrison.

They crossed a small open space and went into the shadows of another thatched hut before they had to stop. The sentry, almost invisible in his black pajama-like uniform, walked his post slowly and methodically. His pitch helmet with its red star was easily visible.

When he passed by them, the two Black Eagles carefully high-stepped their way around the hut to a stack of fifty-gallon drums. Another guard appeared out of the gloom. This one, however, was glancing around. He finally reached a certain point and stopped. Emitting a derisive laugh, he banged on what seemed to be a wooden box.

Both Falconi and Archie knew that would be the POW cage.

The Black Eagles wanted to take the taunting sentry and slit his throat from ear to ear, but that would have put their primary rescue mission in jeopardy. Eventually he tired of his game of teasing the prisoner, and went on to complete his rounds.

Now Falconi led the way. He crawled around the drums with Archie on his heels. When he reached the cage, he stopped. "Hey, buddy!" he whispered. "Don't say anything or make any noise. We're getting you out of there."

The prisoner was silent for a few moments, then he spoke softly. "I already got the slats on that side loose. They'll come apart easy."

Falconi, now with Archie covering him, put his face close so he could make sure the man was an American. When he saw the face in the moonlight, he gasped, "Jesus! Rory Riley!"

"Goddamn!" Major Riley said. "I never thought your ugly mug would look so good, Falconi. Let's get my ass outta here. I think they're planning on moving me tomorrow."

They both worked for the next five minutes to remove the slats. When they were pulled down, Riley crawled out and joined him. He was shirtless and bootless, wearing only tiger-pattern fatigue trousers. Falconi was concerned. "Are you going to be able to travel though the jungle barefoot?"

"What the hell you think I've been doing for the past three months, you dumb shit! I just hope you can keep up with me."

231

Archie made no sound of surprise, but he sent out strong vibes of astonishment. After only a millisecond's delay, he turned and led the other two back across the garrison.

They had to wait for the same guard going out. When the man strolled away into the night, the three Americans slipped back into the jungle.

Now, with the entire Black Eagle detachment, the rest of the escape went into high gear.

CHAPTER 21

Major Rory Riley was an old acquaintance of the Black Eagles'.

It would have been difficult to describe their relationship as a friendly one, but despite the animosity, there was a strong thread of loyalty and mutual respect that had kept Riley from killing any of the Black Eagles and vice-versa during their long and stormy affiliation.

Riley was the commander of a Special Forces "B" camp called Nui Dep. Falconi and his men had spent a lot of time stationed there between missions. There had been quarrels and brawls between the Black Eagles and Green Berets that had finally culminated in an awful situation when Archie Dobbs got drunk out of his mind and stole Major Riley's jeep. That would have been bad enough, but the Black Eagle scout had accidentally run the vehicle into the camp's trash dump, turning it over and breaking the rear axle.

Riley, in his shouting, righteous indignation, had demanded restitution, and had claimed the Black Eagles' most prized possession as payment. This was a refrigerator, and the loss of that priceless beer-cooling item was a bitter blow to Black Eagle prestige and morale. Archie Dobbs, as the direct cause of this deprivation, had lived a life of pure hell for a long time.

But despite all this unpleasantness, not one Black Eagle would have hesitated to risk his life to rescue Rory Riley from the torment of captivity under the Viet Cong. And each knew that Riley would have done the same for them.

Now, squatting in a jungle clearing, Riley was fitted out with an extra pair of boots, donated by Blue Richards, a boonie hat, by Malpractice McCorckel, a shirt, by Buffalo Soldier Culpepper, and Gunnar the Gunner's AK47.

The Norwegian, who had been toting both that assault rifle and his beloved machine gun, was only too glad to get rid of the extra weight.

Riley, happy as hell to be armed and on the loose again, talked and joked with his rescuers. In the meantime, Paulo Garcia was huddled next to the radio, taking down the coded message being broadcast. It was a long one, and by the time he'd signed off, three full pages of his message book were filled with groups of five numbers that had to be decoded.

This would be the commanding officer's job. Although he hated the tedious task, Falconi fully recognized the importance of a timely and accurate deciphering job. This was particularly important when exfiltration, with a myriad coordinating instructions, was in the offing.

It took Falconi twice as long to bring the numbers into legible English as it had for Paulo to write them down. But when he was finished, the final phases of Operation Hellhound were ready to put into effect.

"Gather 'round, guys," he announced. "We've got six hours to meet our aircraft and get lifted out of here."

Archie got up and walked over to sit down beside Falconi. "Do we have to choose the landing zone, sir?"

Falconi shook his head. "Nope. They've picked out one. And I've got good news and bad news about it."

"What's the good news?" Swift Elk asked.

"The good news is that it's only about five kilometers from here," Falconi answered. "In fact, it is a long, straight stretch of that same road we've been raising hell around since we got out here."

"So what's the bad news?" Top Gordon inquired.

"There're North Vietnamese positions on both ends of that portion," Falconi said. "We'll have to make a coordinated assault on both at once."

"Holy shit!" Archie exclaimed. "If one of them attacks fails, we'll all get wasted."

"Then that'll be *real* bad news," Falconi said. "I've already worked out most of the details in my mind, so let's lay this thing out." He looked over at Major Rory Riley. "Care to make any input, Riley?"

Riley shook his head. "No thanks, Falconi. I'm just a guest, so I'll stay out of any family squabbles."

Falconi, already spreading his map out, signaled to his men to gather in closer. "This," he said, "is where we'll be given plenty of glory or buy that goddamned proverbial farm—"

Raoul Luellette, bleary-eyed and half-sick, adjusted the throttles of the C-47 that sat on the apron leading to the runway. The ancient airplane trembled and struggled against both the chocks holding its wheels and the brakes that were held on through the efforts of both Raoul and Chuck Fagin pushing down hard on the rudder pedals.

"How're you feeling?" Fagin asked.

"J'ai mal à la tête," Raoul complained.

Fagin knew just enough French to understand what his companion said. "Your fucking head ought to hurt, you drunken bastard!"

"Sacre!" Raoul exclaimed. "I 'ope I never see the cups of coffee again."

"Looky here, ol' *ami,"* Fagin said. "If I ever need your services when you're drunk again, you can expect the same thing. Except the coffee will be hotter and the shower colder."

"That is another thing I do not like," Raoul said. "That water was freezing off my balls."

"You're sober, ain't you?"

"I am sick!"

"You're gonna fly this frigging airplane, sick or not," Fagin threatened. "And you're gonna fly it right to this fucking point here!" He banged the map on his lap with a pudgy forefinger. "We got to land on this here road and pick up Falconi and the guys. Then we're going to fly straight back here to Peterson Field."

236

"That is enemy territory out there!" Raoul complained.

Fagin repeated himself. "Fly this frigging airplane."

"C'est bon." Raoul relented. "Signal the ground crew to the chocks remove them from the wheels and off the rudders take your feet."

Fagin did as he was told. "Your English gets real shitty when you're mad." He waved to the two Vietnamese air force men out on the concrete.

Now, with the engines fine-tuned and in perfect pitch, the airplane rolled forward to the end of the runway. When Raoul reached the take-off point, he said, "On the rudders your feet!"

While both held the brakes on, the engines were revved to the proper RPM. Then Raoul yelled out, *"Allez!"*

The C-47 began its take-off run, gaining speed until it slowly lifted into the sky. Fagin, anxious and worried, checked the gyro-compass as Raoul turned onto the correct heading.

"Falconi," Fagin said under his breath to himself. "Getting you outta there is gonna take pure, blind, stupid luck!"

Raoul, with pain pounding in his head, gritted his teeth and winced at the bright sunlight streaming in through the windshield. A surge of nausea hit him, but he fought it down and continued flying the plane.

CHAPTER 22

Lieutenant Colonel Robert Falconi quickly glanced at his watch. He turned his head to take a look at his men waiting in the jungle. Top Gordon, Blue Richards, Archie Dobbs, and their guest Major Rory Riley were staring straight at him in anxious apprehension. All tightly gripped their weapons, ready for this next phase of the operation to begin.

Falconi knew that this exact scene was being staged down the road, where another North Vietnamese position was situated. There, Swift Elk, Malpractice, Buffalo Soldier, Paulo, and Gunnar were waiting to launch their own attack.

The sweep hand on the commander's watch swung horribly slowly, it seemed to him, toward the twelve.

Falconi counted off the seconds to himself, "Ten, nine, eight, seven, six, five, four, three, two, one—"

The lieutenant colonel's AK47 belched flame and steel-jacketed slugs that slapped into the Communist roadblock.

Fagin held the microphone in his hand, ready to broadcast or answer any call from Falconi at a second's notice. But he fought the strong desire to raise the Black Eagles and ask them what the hell was going on.

It had been decided that radio silence would be one of the most important elements in the security of the exfiltration. Too much jabbering over the air would arouse enemy listening stations, which would immediately alert their ground units to the presence of unusual activity.

Fagin nudged Raoul and leaned closer. "How're we doing?"

Raoul sighed. His head still felt like a well-used anvil. "We are on course," he yelled back. "Now leave me alone to fly this airplane, eh?"

"All right, all right!" Fagin relented. He glanced out the window for some easily identifiable terrain feature. The CIA case officer saw an elongated mountain that appeared to flow downward to a basin-shaped valley. He anxiously sought it out on the map and quickly found it. They were only fifteen minutes from the waiting point.

The North Vietnamese infantry in the north blockhouse were caught flat-footed by the attack directed on

240

them by Swift Elk.

Gunnar's nimble trigger finger played a roaring symphony of death on the RPK light machine gun, although most of the slugs slapped the small fortification's log walls. But a few of the bullets streaked in through the firing slits, either scoring direct hits on the occupants inside or else ricocheting off the bulkheads before hitting them. Swift Elk, Malpractice, and Buffalo Soldier added their own choruses to the battle's musical program.

Paulo Garcia, taking advantage of all the fire pouring into the enemy position, leaped up and ran across the road to a point where he could dive beneath the NVA's shooting portals and lie out of sight. He pulled one of the fresh grenades lately delivered by Chuck Fagin and waved a signal to Swift Elk.

"Cease fire!" he yelled.

For one solid beat, Paulo was at the mercy of the NVA's weapons.

The shrill whistles of NCOs blew frantically, echoing across the North Vietnamese infantry garrison. This small camp, occupied by a single rifle company, quickly responded to the summons.

There was no shock or surprise at this call to arms.

The sounds of firing down the road had interrupted their afternoon routine ten minutes previously. The men, turning their heads to look in the direction of this disturbance, were combat veterans who recognized shots fired in anger. If there was any puzzlement on their part, it was because the only shots heard were those of their own type of weapons. The higher,

241

sharper discharges of M16s and M60s were noticeably absent from the explosive fusillades bombarding their ears.

Now, fully armed and equipped with bandoleers and grenades, they formed up in platoon formations and waited for whatever their company commander had to tell them. This officer, as experienced in battle as his men, didn't waste time on a lot of words:

"Comrade soldiers!" he exclaimed. "Our signals section has picked up calls of distress from roadblocks south of here. They are under attack by hundreds of imperialist troops. We go to their rescue!"

The nine Black Eagles would have been amused had they known their efforts were so terrifyingly effective that the enemy guessed their numbers at more than ten times the detachment's actual strength. But the sight of a hundred and fifty determined NVA infantry boarding trucks to sweep down on them would have ended any sense of that amusement.

The blockhouse was quickly overtaken by Falconi's team.

The detachment commander had only to pause at the door and insert the business end of his AK47 and end this part of the battle with a few long fire bursts.

Major Rory Riley, with his newly acquired AK47 in hand, rushed past the colonel and inflicted any necessary *coups de grace* on the enemy crew inside.

"Hell, that wasn't so hard," Archie Dobbs said, moving to the other side of the small fortification to keep a lookout for any interlopers.

"Yeah," Blue said, joining him. "I hope things is

goin' jest as good fer Mr. Swift Elk and the boys."

Sergeant Major Top Gordon, the remnants of his last cigar clenched tightly between his teeth, came around the blockhouse. "Let's move up the road about ten or fifteen meters," he ordered. "Just in case—"

His words were cut off by the appearance of several truckloads of NVA.

"This is the place," Fagin announced loudly. He held up his map for Raoul to see. "We're here."

"Right," Raoul said. He pressed the left rudder and turned the wheel in that direction. The little transport responded faithfully, going into a tight but gentle turn. "Tell me, Fagin. 'ow long we orbit this area, eh?"

"Until Falconi tells us to come in and pick them up," Fagin replied.

Raoul grinned. "Or we run out of the gasoline. Or we lose the power. Or we get shot down. Or—"

"Shut up!"

"*Sacre!*" Raoul said in a huff. "You are such the *sensitif!*"

Paulo, his injured hand holding onto his AK47, shoved the grenade through the roadblock's firing slit. He quickly ducked down. A muffled explosion, made half again more than its normal strength because of the confinement of the building, rocked the structure.

All firing and activity inside ceased.

Paulo, now holding his weapon at the ready, checked the interior. He stepped back and waved to Swift Elk. "We're secured, sir."

243

"Right," Swift Elk acknowledged. He got his Prick-Six radio. "Falcon, this is Horse. We have taken our objective. Over."

A couple of moments elapsed before Falconi's labored voice came over the receiver. "Horse, so have we. But company has come calling. Get your butts down here."

Swift Elk hollered at his men and they double-timed down the road toward the sound of a firefight building up into a roaring intensity. It took them a full five minutes before they finally joined the others. The Sioux officer sent his men to fighting positions with curt gestures, then he dove in beside Falconi.

"What's the situation, sir?"

"I'd estimate we're getting hit by a company-sized unit of NVA," Falconi said. "They're a little hesitant, so the sons-of-bitches haven't figured out there's not even a dozen of us here. But when they do, it'll be curtains."

"What's the situation on the exfiltration aircraft?" Swift Elk asked.

"He should be in orbit waiting for us to call him in," Falconi said. "And now that we're all together, that's exactly what I'm going to do."

A sudden flurry of shots smacked around them, making the two officers instinctively duck their heads.

"Sir," Swift Elk said. "You'd better make that radio call *now!*"

Falconi nodded. He grabbed his radio and hit the transmit button. "Irish, this is Eagle. Come in now. The area outside the landing spot on the road is not secure. Make your approach south to north. Hit the deck and brake hard. We'll be running up to catch you. Out!"

244

The NVA attack built up on the right side of the line. Falconi yelled out, "Blue, Paulo! Get over there and help those guys. Where the hell is Gunnar?"

The Minnesotan's voice, close by, quickly answered. "I read you, sir. Me and Prinsesse will help out."

The sudden explosion of gunfire in that section of the fight was heralded by the surprise appearance of the C-47. The airplane came in so low that dust flew up from the shoulders of the road as it roared in over them and touched down.

The Black Eagles couldn't see them, but both Raoul and Fagin were standing on the brakes while the reversed props blasted away in the opposite direction.

"Grenades, goddamnit!" Falconi bellowed. "Everyone swinging dick heave two of the damned things. Now! *Now!*"

In the space of a few heartbeats, eighteen well-thrown hand grenades, launched by muscular arms, lobbed high through the air and bounced onto the ground on both sides of the road.

When the detonations began, the Black Eagles cut and ran.

Fagin, leaning out the door, gestured them to hurry. As they reached him, the CIA man reached down and literally pulled the Black Eagles into the troop compartment.

Falconi, the last man, held out his hand. Incoming rounds kicked up the dirt around his feet, until Fagin, his pudgy body making one last effort, tugged with all the strength left in him.

Both men tumbled onto the deck of the aircraft. Raoul, peering back from the cockpit, pushed the throttles forward. Pings and ricochets of incoming enemy fire enveloped the plane, causing a couple of control wires to pop.

The controls became sluggish, but Raoul nursed the wheel and rudders until the faithful Dakota responded. She quickly picked up speed until she was airborne. The plane banked, slightly, gained more altitude, and headed south for home.

Falconi got to his feet. He looked around and checked his men. All nine, plus Major Rory Riley and Chuck Fagin, were sprawled around him.

"Gentlemen," he loudly announced, "I hereby adjourn Operation Hellhound!"

CHAPTER 23

Brigadier General James Taggart, the Ridgeway cap set straight on his shaven head, watched the C-47 taxi up to where he stood on the runway of Peterson Field.

The general waited until the engines were cut, before he walked up to the aircraft's door. When it opened, Archie Dobbs jumped out onto the ground. He was quickly followed by the others, who stared in unhappy anticipation at the high-ranking officer and his silent greeting.

Finally Rory Riley and Chuck Fagin appeared. They stepped down. Taggart motioned to Riley. "Get your butt over to G2 for debriefing. There's a jeep on the other side of the hangar to take you there."

Riley, thinking this was only a bit better than his

treatment by his former captors, the Viet Cong, saluted. "Yes, sir."

Taggart turned to Falconi. "Come here!"

Falconi stepped up and snapped to attention. He rendered a sharp salute. "Sir, Lieutenant Colonel Falconi reporting as ordered."

"The hell if you are!" Taggart yelled. "If you were 'reporting as ordered' you'd been back here weeks ago." He looked over Falconi's shoulder at Top Gordon. "You're the sergeant major?"

"Yes, sir!" Top answered.

"Then put that gang of pirates at attention when a goddamned general is in the area!" Taggart ordered.

Top barked the orders and formed the men up in a proper formation. They stood rigid and unmoving in the hot sun.

"You probably figure you really got one over on me, Falconi," Taggart hissed. "But you haven't, goddamn you! And you're not home yet, either. You see that Chinook helicopter over there?" He again looked at the men. "You people look at that chopper, too! Do you see it?"

"Yes, sir!" they responded.

"Good, because you're going to get your asses on the goddamned thing and fly out to where the hell we should've kept you in the first place." The general smiled. "Since you seem to play your cards in such a way that you stay away from Peterson Field and Saigon so long, you'll be happy to know that you're moving back to your old billets—Camp Nui Dep!"

A collective moan arose from the group. This was the Special Forces "B" Detachment camp where they had spent so much time. Major Rory Riley was the

248

official commander of the place, and his presence there, combined with the monotony and dreariness of the environment, always led to unpleasant occurrences in their lives.

"Oh, sergeant major!" Taggart sang out in sarcastic glee. "Before you put your men on the Chinook, why don't you give them an 'about-face' command?"

"Sir?" Top asked, puzzled.

"That way they'll be able to see through the fence into Saigon. That'll be their last glimpse of fleshpots, bars, and other forms of licentious diversion that they love so much," Taggart said. He took another salute from Falconi and walked away.

"Camp Nui Dep!" Top swore under his breath. But he turned and faced the men. "Black Eagle Detachment!" he commanded. "About-*face!*"

Archie swore under his breath. "I hope Major Rory Riley remembers we rescued him from a VC prison cage."

"Are you jiving, man?" Buffalo Soldier Calvin Culpepper remarked. "That man is gonna bring hot, scalding pee all over us out there."

"Amen!" Blue agreed with a moan.

Once more Sergeant Top Gordon ordered an about-face. "Okay, guys," he said with an uncharacteristic note of sympathy in his voice. "When I give the word, fall out on that chopper the general pointed out to us. We're Nui Dep bound!" He took a deep breath and shouted, "Fall out!"

Silent and downcast, the Black Eagles headed for whatever adventure that hellhole had for them.

249

EPILOGUE

The young Viet Cong guerrilla sat comfortably in his perch in the high tree.

His position, secured by expertly tied planking, was roomy and made his task easier. He could plainly make out the entire layout of Camp Nui Dep. Its mortar positions, entrenchments, various dugouts and bunkers, and the landing strip were clearly visible to him. The VC worked diligently on his project, carefully sketching all these details. His natural talents were so great that the drawing was almost to scale.

Now, after more than a week of tending to this task, he was in its final phases. The only thing left to do was to put in the ranges of the camp's various points for the benefit of the mortar crews who would be servicing the

Soviet M1937 82 millimeter mortars that would rain down a roaring hell of explosive and flying shards of steel on the camp.

A rumble of thunder in the sky behind him caught his attention. The Viet Cong broke his concentration long enough to look back at it. The black monsoon clouds were building up fast over Southeast Asia.

He looked back at Camp Nui Dep. The inhabitants of the garrison would never expect an attack, much less the murderous one planned for them, during this season of wind and rains.

He smiled to himself as he put the finishing touches on his map.

THE SURVIVALIST SERIES
by Jerry Ahern